Love,

Roger

By Charles Webb

The Graduate
Love, Roger

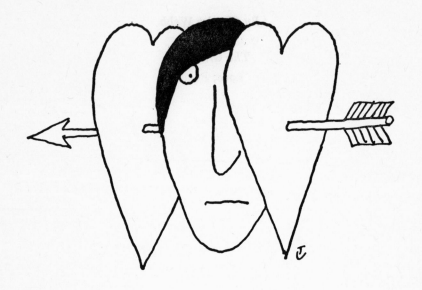

Love,
Roger

CHARLES WEBB

HOUGHTON MIFFLIN COMPANY

BOSTON 1969

frontispiece drawing by
Tomi Ungerer

First Printing   w

Copyright © 1969 by Charles Webb

*Library of Congress
Catalog Card Number: 69–15031*

Printed in the United States of America

To Eve

Love,

Roger

1

THE REASON I had to go to Filene's was to pick up some stationery with my name on it, which I had ordered a few weeks before. During the middle of the afternoon I called up to find out if the stationery was ready, and I should have found out how late the store was open.

I got there just as it was closing. On the other side of the glass doors a man was turning a key in the lock. "Sir?" I said.

He pointed at some letters on the door that said the store closed at five-thirty, then turned and started walking away.

"Sir?" I said again, putting my face up to the crack between the doors.

He stopped, turned around and came partway back toward the doors. "We're closed," he said.

"I thought you were open till six."

"Five-thirty."

I pointed over to one of the counters inside where a woman was being handed a package. "I see a customer in there," I said.

The man looked over at her, then back at me. "She's just leaving."

The woman took her bag and started over toward the door. As she approached, the man opened it for her, then stood and held it as she walked out.

"I have some stationery to pick up," I said. "I could just run in, pick it up, then run out."

"We're closed," he said.

I stepped nearer and moved my shoe ahead so the door stuck on it. "I had a letter to write tonight. I wanted to be able to write it on personalized stationery."

The man looked down at my shoe.

I pointed in at another man who was at a counter receiving a package from a clerk. "I see another customer," I said. "Could I just run in and out?"

The man stepped aside.

I hurried in past him and walked across the floor to an escalator and started up. On the mezzanine I got off and started toward the stationery counter. Just as I reached it the man behind stepped out, putting on his coat. "Hi," I said.

"Hello." He started walking past me.

"They were kind enough to let me in down below," I said. "I have some stationery to pick up; I called earlier and it's ready."

"We're closed," he said.

"But they were good enough to let me in down below," I said. "I have a letter it's quite important for me to write tonight."

He looked at me a moment, then walked back behind the counter. "What's your name."

"Hart, Roger," I said.

He opened a drawer in a wall of drawers on the other side of the counter. "What is it?"

"Roger Hart."

"Which comes first."

"Roger does."

He closed the first drawer and opened another. Then he lifted out a box of stationery and turned around. "That's four dollars and fifty cents," he said. "If you had the right change it would save me unlocking the register."

I removed my wallet and took out four dollar bills, then reached into my pocket and brought out a handful of change. "I have it."

"I'm glad."

I gave him the money.

"Would you like a bag for it?" he said, handing me the stationery box.

"I don't need one." I turned around and started walking away.

There were two pieces of scotch tape keeping the box closed. I broke them with my fingernail as I was walking along and lifted the lid off the box. On top were the sheets of stationery with my name and my address at the top of them. I picked up the sheets to look at the envelopes underneath. They also had my name and my address on them, on the flap, in black lettering. I closed the box and looked up.

I was walking toward some elevators. One of the elevator doors was open and two saleswomen were stepping through it. No one else was left on the floor. I hurried on toward the elevator but before I could get there the door closed.

Beside the elevators was a door with a red light bulb over it and a STAIRS sign above it. I walked to the door and pulled it open and walked through into the stairwell.

Before that moment I have never before seen a girl faint. Melinda Gray was the first, and she fainted right there before my eyes. Out of the corner of my eye I noticed her coming down the stairs above me. I didn't look at her but started across the landing leading to the stairs to the first floor and it was just as I stepped down on the top stair that I heard her make a sighing noise and turned around to see her crumple against the wall. One of her hands was up over her face. She slid slowly down along the side of the wall, then rolled down the stairs.

At first I didn't know what to do except look at her. She was lying on her side with her cheek on the concrete. Finally I walked back toward her and bent over her for a few moments to look at her face. Then I pulled open the door beside us and stepped partway back through it. There was no one in sight. "Hello?" I said. There was no answer. "Hello!" It was perfectly still in the store; the only noise was from traffic that was passing by below on the street, the noise coming up and into the stairwell through a small ventilation window beside the stairs. I stepped back out onto the landing and let the door shut. The girl's eyes were closed and she still hadn't moved. I got down on my knees beside her and set my box of stationery on the concrete. Then I reached out and put my hand on her shoulder. Very slowly I turned her over on her back, then moved my head down and put my ear against her chest. I continued to hear only the traffic noises coming up from below. "Oh God," I said. I lifted my head up again, then quickly picked up one of her wrists and put my finger on it till I felt the pulse. "She's alive," I said. I stood up. "She's alive." I looked around for a moment, then ran up to the next landing. I looked around again and ran up another flight. There were two rest rooms, then a door leading back into the store. I pulled it open. "Hello!" There was no one in sight. A section called "Gift Boutique" stood in front of me, and displays of dresses stretched out across the floor. "Can anyone hear me!" Again there was no answer. "There's a girl on the landing who's fainted!" I waited a moment, then turned around and started back down the stairs. Then I stopped and hurried back up and into the men's room. There was no light on but some gray light was still coming in through an opaque window in the wall. I went to the sink and turned on a faucet, then yanked several paper towels down out of the towel dispenser over the sink and held them under the water. When they were soaked I carried them down the stairs.

The girl still hadn't moved. I got down on my knees and began patting the wet towels against her forehead and cheeks. "Wake up," I said. I patted them around under her chin and over her eyes, but her eyes didn't open. I glanced at the door a moment, then looked down at her face again and finally lowered my head until my mouth was just over hers. I opened her mouth with my hands and put my lips against hers, then took a deep breath and breathed out into her mouth, keeping my lips tightly against hers, so the air was forced down into her chest. I could feel her breasts pressing upward against my chest, then her head moved and she pulled her mouth away from mine. "She's coming to," I said. I pushed my arms under her body, then braced my back against the wall and lifted her up slowly. Her legs hung down on one side of me and her head hung loosely down on the other. I carried her slowly up the stairs past the rest rooms and to the door leading into the store. I tried several times to open it with my thumb but it was a heavy steel door and each time it went closed again before I could get my foot in it. Finally I hoisted the girl up so she was resting over my shoulder, opened the door and carried her through.

I carried her past the gift shop and toward a bathroom display and then into the linen section. There were several single beds in a row and then some large ones, aisles between them. Some had bedspreads and pillows on them; some had just the blue-and-white or pink-and-white striped mattresses. I eased the girl down on her back on one of the beds, then sat down beside her. I looked at my watch. It was just after six. I put my head down onto her chest and listened to her heartbeats for a few moments, then sat up again. She had long black hair which was spread out on the pillow beside her head. The lipstick she was wearing was light pink color, and looked kind of whitish on her lips. Her mouth was open slightly and she was breathing through her mouth, her head resting a little bit to the side. I glanced down at one of her hands, then at the other. There were no rings on any of her fingers. She had a short corduroy skirt on, and a heavy green sweater. I looked at my watch again, then back up at her face, then decided to try and revive her again.

This time I got up on my knees and moved her face slightly so it was facing upward. "Hello," I said. She didn't move. I took ahold of her chin and shook her head slightly. "Hello?" I tapped against her cheek. Finally I bent down over her and put my mouth against hers. I had forgotten to take a deep breath first so I had to lift my head up slightly, take the breath, then put it down again and breathe out into her mouth. I raised my head again for another breath of air, then lowered it. It was just in the middle of one of the times that I was breathing air into her mouth that she woke up. I felt her eyelashes brush my cheek and I stopped breathing. I didn't know whether to continue breathing the rest of the air into her mouth now that she was awake or not. For several moments neither of us moved. Then I raised my head. She lay in the same position, her mouth still open, and looked up at me. I stood up, then pointed off across the room to the door leading to the stairwell.

"What's happening," she said.

"That door," I said. "You fainted as you came down the stairs. I carried you in here."

She glanced down at the bedspread a moment, then back at me. "Who are you."

"Roger Hart," I said. "You fainted as you were coming down the stairs."

"I did?"

"You passed out," I said. "I didn't know what else to do."

She raised her head up slightly from the pillow. "What were you doing to me just now."

"Trying to bring you around."

"By kissing me?"

"I was administering mouth-to-mouth resuscitation," I said. "If I hadn't you'd still be unconscious."

She looked at me a moment longer, then raised herself up on her elbows. "Where am I."

"Filene's."

She turned her head and looked over at a breakfast room table. "Where is everybody."

"It's closed."

"The store's closed?"

"Yes." I stood another moment watching her, then took a step toward the bed. "What about your head," I said.

"What about it."

"You hit it," I said. "You were coming down the stairs. You came tumbling down. You hit your face."

She reached up to run her fingers over one of her cheeks. "I feel no pain in my face."

"Other side."

She ran her fingers over the other side.

"There aren't any marks," I said. "It was a lucky fall."

She looked up at me again. "You say I tumbled down."

"Yes." I raised my hand up and brought it down. "Sort of slowly. I didn't see the whole fall. I heard a noise; I turned around and you were sort of tumbling down."

"Hurtling?"

"No no. Just tumbling very slowly. You were almost at the bottom of the stairs when it happened."

"And what did you do."

"I turned around."

"You didn't try and break my fall."

"I couldn't," I said. I indicated a space with my hands. "You were here. I was here. I heard a noise and turned around and you were down."

"What noise."

"A fainting noise."

The girl ran her hand back through her hair, then sat up on the bed. "So," she said.

"We'd better get organized," I said. "You're sure you're all right."

"I think so."

"Then maybe we could each take different floors and search for a clerk."

"What are you."

"I'm a customer," I said.

"Will you get me a drink of water?"

She got up from the bed and walked along through the aisle between some of the beds until she came to a dining room table. It was fully set, a large bowl of plastic fruit in the center. At the top of each place setting was a large purple goblet. She picked one up and carried it back to where I was standing.

"What's this," I said.

She handed it to me. "I want my drink of water in it."

"What for."

She walked past me and seated herself on the edge of the bed. "If you please," she said.

"But why."

"I like the glass," she said. "I like the pattern; I like the kind of glass it is; I would like to drink out of it."

I looked at her a moment longer, then turned and started

back toward the door leading out onto the stairs. "There's a rest room on the landing."

"Thank you."

"I'll get the water." I carried the goblet across the floor, then through the door and into the men's room. After filling it I walked back to the landing where my stationery box was, picked it up, then returned to the girl who was still sitting on the bed. I handed her the water.

"Thank you."

"You're welcome."

She tipped it up to her lips and drank about half of it, then she lowered it and held the glass in her lap. "What's that," she said, looking at the box in my hand.

"It's stationery."

She raised the glass to her lips again and took another swallow.

"That's why I was here," I said. "To pick it up. I left it down on the landing when you fainted."

She lowered the glass again. "Just plain stationery?" she said.

"Yes. It's a plain kind."

"Not with your name on it or anything."

"My name," I said. "Yes."

"What is it."

"My name? Roger Hart."

"I'm Melinda."

"Oh."

"Can I see the stationery?"

"Sure." I lifted off the top of the box.

"I've never had my name on stationery," Melinda said.

"I hadn't either." I turned the box around and held it out in front of her. "It came out well."

"It did."

"Black print."

"Yes." She pointed at the lettering at the top of the first sheet. "Roger Hart."

"Yes."

"Then your address under there."

"Yes."

She looked up at me. "It's nice," she said.

"I like it too." I returned the top back onto the box. "I'm looking forward to using it. I had a letter to write tonight. I was looking forward to using it for that."

"A business letter?"

"No."

"Private."

"Yes." I squeezed the top tightly onto the box and lowered it to my side again. "Let's see now."

"I guess you don't want to talk about it."

"About what."

"The letter."

"Oh," I said. I glanced down at the box of stationery again. "It's not that. It's just that it seems more important to talk about the immediate situation instead."

"Which is what."

"Which is how we're going to get out of here," I said. I looked off across the floor and over the tops of the furniture displays. "If there were a clerk on this floor I'm sure we would have seen him by now."

"I'm sure of it."

"What about my plan then."

Melinda stood up from the edge of the bed. "What's that."

"Fan out," I said. "Take different floors and see if we can find one."

"What about my purse," Melinda said. She bent over and looked under the bed.

"What purse."

"I had it in my hand."

"When."

"When I fainted."

I looked down at the corner of the bed. "I'm sure you didn't."

Melinda got down on one knee. "You didn't see it."

"You didn't have it," I said. "You fell down the stairs. I was right there. There was no purse."

She looked up at me but didn't say anything.

"I would have seen it," I said.

"Where is it."

"What?"

"Three or four dollars in cash," she said. "I don't care so much about that, but the papers. My social security card."

"Look," I said, "it wasn't there; I would have seen it."

Melinda got up and started walking toward the door. "This is serious," she said.

I followed her.

"You can have the money," she said, "but I don't know what I'll do without my papers."

"What are you trying to say."

"I'm trying to say you can keep the money."

"You're saying you think I took your purse?"

"You can even have the purse itself," she said.

"Stop a minute."

She continued toward the door.

"Wait." I reached out for her hand. She stopped when I took it and turned around.

"What are you saying," I said.

"I'm saying I need my purse."

"Yes," I said, "but you're saying I took it."

"Who else could have."

I looked down at her hand, then let go of it. "No one else could have," I said. "I'm telling you there was no purse in your hand when you fainted."

"There was when I started fainting," she said. "There might not have been when I finished."

"There wasn't when you started."

She turned around and began toward the door again.

"You weren't there when I started."

"I was right on the landing, four yards away."

"That wasn't where I started."

"Where did you start."

"Up above," she said. "Right outside the doorway of the personnel office. I came out and started down the stairs and started fainting. I thought I could get all the way down and out onto the street for some fresh air but I didn't make it." She pulled open the door under the word STAIRS.

We turned around a banister at the top of the first flight and started up the next. About twelve steps up, over at the side and lying upside down, was a black purse.

"Let me get it." I hurried ahead of her and picked it up and handed it to her. She pulled open a zipper across the top of it, opened it and pulled out a red plastic wallet. She opened it and ran her thumb through several dollar bills. Then she pulled open a compartment of plastic envelopes and looked through them.

"Is everything there?"

"I think so." She put the wallet back in the purse, then looked down into the purse, shook it up and down a few times as she was looking into it, then zipped it shut again. "It's all right," she said. "I'm sorry I accused you."

"Don't worry."

"I shouldn't have done it," she said. "I should have known anyone who would stop and help me and give me mouth-to-mouth resuscitation wouldn't be a person to steal my purse."

"You were panicked about it."

"I was."

"I can understand that."

"I was up there," she said, pointing up at a doorway at the top of the stairs. "That's personnel. They told me to come over and I'd have a job. Then when I came over they told me I couldn't have it. I knew as soon as they told me I was going to faint. I thought if I could get down to the street, though, that I might not. So I started down. But as you know I didn't make it to the street."

"No."

It was very dim in the stairwell. There was a grimy small glass window in the wall just above where I was standing and the only light that was coming in was coming in through that. I was standing two stairs above Melinda. "You needed a job," I said.

"That's why I was here."

"And you say they told you to come, and then when you got here they told you they didn't have it."

"There was a want ad," she said. "I called up and they said they would hire me if I'd had previous experience, which I had, but when I got here they said they wouldn't hire me."

"Rough," I said.

"I had my hopes up."

"I can see that."

"I mean after they said I could go ahead and start work if I came over here I got my hopes up."

"Of course."

"Then I sat down and waited about an hour and the woman came and said it would be impossible for me to work here."

"Why."

"She didn't say."

I nodded.

"But when she said that I knew I was going to faint."

"Well look."

"I didn't want to argue."

"No."

"You can argue and argue with these people. What's the point; they hold the strings of power."

"What you're saying here though," I said, "is that you need a job."

"I have four dollars in my wallet."

"And you need a job."

"Yes."

"And you've been trying for a while?"

"Ten days."

"Well," I said, "I mean I'm sure you could get one. Is that why you fainted?"

"Why."

"Did you faint because you can't get a job?"

"I fainted because I'm at the end of my rope."

I looked down at my wristwatch, then back at Melinda. "I work in a travel agency," I said. "It's the Becker Travel Agency. If you come by tomorrow morning I could maybe make a few phone calls. I'm not promising anything, but if you come by I could try."

"I will."

I nodded. "Good."

"Becker."

"The Becker Travel Agency."

She unzipped her purse again and began rummaging around in it.

"It's very near here," I said. "Right opposite the Statler Hilton."

She stopped rummaging. "It couldn't be."

"Not right opposite," I said. "Sort of down across the street. Down the block a little."

She lifted a pencil up out of the purse. "I would have noticed if it was directly across," she said. "That's where I'm staying."

"Oh."

"Yes." She reached into her purse again and removed her wallet. She pulled it open and pulled one of the cards out of its plastic window. "Becker," she said, sitting down on the step.

"Yes."

She put the card up against the wall and began writing on it.

"You realize that's your social security card."

"I can erase it later," she said. "What's your address."

"Five hundred and ten St. James."

She wrote for a few more seconds, then dropped the pencil and the card into her purse and stood. "I'll come over in the morning," she said, "if that's all right."

"Fine," I said. "I'm not promising anything but I'll do everything I can."

"Thank you." She turned and started down the stairs. At the landing she turned and started down the next flight.

I cleared my throat. "Melinda?"

"Yes?"

There was a silence. "Where were you going."

"Down."

"To find a clerk?"

"Sure."

"Good," I said, starting down, "let's try that."

I walked past her and pushed open the door leading back out onto the floor. "Why don't I start here," I said. "Someone might have come up while we were on the stairs."

She walked up to the door and looked. "How would he have come up," she said, "if not by the stairs."

"Many ways," I said. "He could have come up the escalator."

"Oh yes."

"So."

"Right."

"You could take the next floor down, then we could meet on the ground floor."

"Good," she said.

I walked in through the door and started past the bathroom displays toward the other side of the floor. When I had gotten to the opposite side I turned and started walking toward another wall. Then I stopped and turned around and noticed, way back across the floor, that Melinda was still standing halfway in the doorway. "What's wrong!"

She called something but I couldn't hear.

I cupped my hand beside my mouth, "I can't hear."

She let the door close behind her and started toward me. "What's wrong," I said as she approached.

"I couldn't hear you from back there."

"But what's wrong," I said. "Why didn't you fan out."

She walked past several tables covered with lamps and came up to where I was standing. "It's too far," she said. "I couldn't understand what you were saying."

"I know that," I said, "but why didn't you go down to the next floor."

"Where?"

"The next floor down; to look for someone."

She looked at me a moment but didn't answer.

"The plan?" I said. "To fan out and find someone?"

"Yes?"

"Well what about it."

"What about it," she said.

"That's what I'm saying."

Beside us was a green chair made of canvas slung over a metal framework, sunk down in a basket. Melinda looked at it a moment, then eased herself down into it. "I think it needs more thought," she said.

"What does."

"The plan," she said. She reached forward and scratched one of her ankles.

"It's a simple plan," I said. "Just find out if there's someone in the building who can let us out."

"You'd think there would be." She looked up at me and pushed some hair away from one of her eyes. "All this valuable merchandise; you wouldn't think they'd take chances."

"That's it."

"Theft."

"Yes."

"Yes." She looked at one of her feet and let the hair fall over her eye again. "But I don't think the plan's practical. As far as locating a clerk or night watchman. The way we were going about it."

"I can't think of any other way."

"Than fanning out."

"There might be other ways," I said. "I can't think of any faster way."

Melinda held out her hand. "May I see the box?"

"What's that."

"The stationery box."

I looked down at the box a moment, then at her hand, then handed it to her.

"Thank you." She opened it again and held it up so that more light fell on the top sheet of stationery. "How did you happen to pick this particular pattern."

"That style?"

"Yes."

"I don't know," I said. "They had a book of different styles, colors. I just picked that one."

"It's nice."

"Thank you; I like it."

"I may get myself some stationery made up," she said, lifting up the top sheets to look at the envelopes beneath them. "I never really thought I'd want to but I can see from this that it might be a good thing to have." She let the sheets of stationery fall back over the envelopes. "For the person receiving the letter it would also be good," she said. "They wouldn't have to read all the way to the end to find out who wrote it." She handed it back, then pushed the hair back along the sides of her head with both hands and smiled up at me.

"About this fanning out," I said. "Instead of that, why don't we stay together instead so when we find him we'll both be there and won't have to hunt around for the other."

"Good idea."

"Let's do that then."

"I'll catch my breath," she said, "then we'll do it." She picked her purse up from the floor and set it in her lap. I stood awhile longer, holding the stationery at my side, then I lifted my wrist to look at my watch. "What time is it," she said.

"Going on six-thirty," I said. "I haven't eaten of course."

"I haven't either." She tilted her head back and looked up at the ceiling. "Did you have a dinner engagement?"

"Me?"

"Yes."

"I didn't have an engagement," I said, "but I usually eat around six."

"That's a good time to do it."

"I get hungry then."

"I usually eat around six-forty-five or seven. Sometimes later."

Melinda sat a moment longer, then leaned forward and put her hands on the edge of the chair and pushed herself to her feet. "If you're hungry," she said, "we'd better find someone."

I started back toward an escalator. "We can just walk down."

We passed the beds again and then got to the head of one of the escalators. "Go ahead."

"Thank you."

We walked down the metal stairs to the bottom. Just at the bottom were several racks of dresses with signs over them that said they were on sale. There was a mannequin on a stand wearing a green dress. Melinda went up to it and felt the hem of the dress. "We could just walk around," I said. "I can't think of any other way."

"That's the only way."

We walked past the dress racks and past a counter of hats and to a counter running along one of the walls.

"Now where," Melinda said.

I looked one way down the counter, then the other. "Nobody."

"Maybe there's a watchman with a special room," Melinda said.

"In the basement?"

I looked down through the top of the glass counter we were standing beside and at some rings, then gestured back toward the escalators. "Let's go down to the basement." I started back toward the escalator and Melinda followed.

"I don't see any sign of a person," she said, looking over the floor.

"I don't either."

"So," she said, "what shall we do next."

"The basement."

"Right."

There was a large display of men in plaid coats standing amidst camping equipment just at the foot of the escalator. I walked several yards to the side so I could look around it and at the doorway that led to the stairs. "That might be the best bet," I said, pointing at it.

"What's that."

"The stairway there," I said. "It might take us down to the basement."

"Good."

I walked past a large khaki tent and toward the side of the room. When I got to the door I opened it and let Melinda go through ahead of me. There were some stairs leading upward but none leading down. "They don't have one," she said.

"They might," I said. "This isn't the way to get to it." I turned around and held the door open again. Melinda walked past me and through it. As she was passing by me I noticed for the first time that in her ear was a small gold earring that hadn't been there before when I had carried her to the bed. I looked at it as her head went by, then she stopped and turned around. "Now what," she said.

There was another small gold earring in her other ear. She turned around and walked past the mannequin of a man dressed in high rubber boots, who was smiling, holding a large fishnet in his hand with a plastic trout in it. "Melinda?" I said.

She stopped just on the other side of the mannequin. "Yes?"

"Just one thing I wanted to say," I said. "I don't want you to think I'm a prude. I just want to say that you realize it's illegal for us to be in here at this time."

"But it's not our fault."

"I know," I said, "but it's private property."

She looked at me a moment, the two gold circles jiggling in her ears.

"I mean it wasn't our fault," I said, "but nonetheless, we are in here and there is a possibility someone might not believe it was by accident that we got locked in."

"We'll tell them I fainted."

"I know," I said. "And I hope they'll believe us, but if they thought we were doing anything funny in here it might mean trouble for us and embarrassment and so forth."

She continued looking at me, tilting her head slightly so that the earring on her left ear hung down and out an inch or so from the side of her head.

"What I'm trying to say is," I said, pointing at the earring, "that I remember distinctly you didn't have those on when you fainted."

"What's that."

"I'm not a prude," I said, "and when I was younger I might have swiped a nickel candy at the Five and Ten but the point is we're in here illegally in the first place and something like that could make it very embarrassing for us and rouse suspicions and so forth."

Melinda lifted one of her arms up and took a hold of an earring. "These?"

"Yes."

"Do you like them?"

"Like them what."

"Do you like them on me. I don't usually wear jewelry. When I do I like to keep it simple."

"I may be mistaken," I said. "Did you have them all along?"

"I've had them all along since we left the second floor."

"That's what I thought."

"The jewelry department. Where they had those rings."

"Right," I said, "well as I mentioned before, when I was a kid, I might have pocketed a penny candy from the Dime Store on a Saturday morning. I'm not a righteous Richard, but if we do come across the watchman and he notices those it could get very embarrassing for the two of us."

"You want me to take them back now," she said.

"It's just if we happen to find the watchman . . ."

"Yes."

"You'd have them on," I said, "and he'd see them."

She reached up to feel the other one. "How about this," she said, "when we see him, as we're going up to him, I'll take them off, quickly."

"And then what."

"Leave them here."

"In the store."

"Yes," she said. "I'm not sure I would really have to take them back. I'm sure a clerk would find them and get them back to the right department." She pulled the two earrings down off her ears. "I can just remove them like that before the watchman sees them."

"Were you planning to leave them?"

"Where."

"Were you planning to leave them in the store."

She pinched one back onto the lobe of her ear. "I hadn't really thought about it."

"When you picked them up and put them on," I said, "you weren't planning to take them out with you?"

"I just felt like wearing them awhile," she said. "I hadn't really thought very far ahead." She fixed the other one in place on the other lobe.

"I'm sorry then," I said.

"About what."

"About accusing you."

"Oh," she said. "Don't worry about it. Let's find the watchman."

I turned around. "I think I'm edgy," I said.

"I don't blame you."

We walked past the tent and past a family of mannequins on a patch of plastic grass on the other side of the tent who were gathered around a barbecue where five plastic trout were cooking over an orange paper flame.

"I mean I realize it's silly to be edgy," I said. "The worst that could happen would be that we'd have to wait till they opened in the morning."

"Wait a minute," Melinda said. She walked ahead of me into the tunnel, then through it. "Come in here."

"Where." I followed her into the tunnel. Just after she said it a light went on in a room off to the left. Melinda was at the far end holding the end of a string that went up to a light at the top.

"A snack bar," I said.

"I remembered it from earlier; I had some coffee here before going up about the job."

I walked in through the door.

Inside was a counter with stools in front of it and a refrigerator and a griddle on the other side. "If worse comes to worst," Melinda said, "we won't starve." She walked around to the other side of the counter and pulled open the refrigerator. "Do you like hamburgers?"

"I like them," I said, "but I don't know about eating them here."

"Eggs?"

"I like eggs."

She reached in and pulled out an egg. "Which do you like better: eggs or hamburgers."

"How about this," I said. "If there's no one maybe we could call the police."

She put the egg back in the icebox. "Then what."

"Just call them and ask for suggestions."

She closed the icebox door. "Do what you want," she said. "It's getting on toward my dinnertime so I might fix myself something before too long." She walked over to the griddle and turned one of its knobs. A jet of blue gas flared up underneath.

"They could probably get ahold of the owner of the store and the owner could come down and let us out."

"You don't want to eat here then," Melinda said, turning off the knob.

"I don't really think it's that good an idea," I said. "No."

She walked back to the icebox and opened it again. "What if I did."

"Ate here?"

"What if I fixed myself a cheeseburger. Would that be upsetting to you?"

I gestured at the griddle. "Go ahead."

"I may." She reached into the refrigerator and removed a meat patty on a small sheet of paper, then carried it over to the griddle, laid it on the metal and peeled off the paper. Then she turned the knob again.

"What about payment," I said.

"What's that."

"What's payment?"

She crumpled the small square of paper and dropped it in a wastebasket on the floor. "Oh. Payment." She removed a menu from between a sugar holder and a napkin dispenser on the counter and opened it. She ran her eyes down one side and then down the other. "Sixty-five cents for a cheeseburger." She glanced over at a tall pie holder at the end of the counter, then back at the menu. "Thirty-five for a piece of pie if I have one, then fifteen for a Coke." She closed the menu and returned it between the sugar container and the napkin dispenser. "How much does that come to. A dollar twenty?"

"A dollar fifteen."

She walked back to the refrigerator. "A dollar fifteen." She reached in and brought out a plastic container filled with lettuce. "Are you sure I can't fix you one?"

"What will you do," I said, "just leave the money on the counter?"

"I thought I would."

"You don't think it might be odd for the waitress to come in in the morning and find money on the counter."

Melinda set the container of lettuce on a shelf beside the griddle. "It might be odd," she said. "I think she'll be able to cope with it though."

"What if the watchman shows up."

"Now?"

"While we're eating."

"I suppose that's a chance we take," she said. "Can I make you a cheeseburger?"

I reached into my pocket and pulled out some change. I looked at it a moment, then put it back. "Yes please."

"You can afford it."

"I can," I said. "I just wanted to make sure I had the correct change."

Melinda walked back to the icebox. "Why don't you have a seat."

"Thank you." I walked over to the center stool, seated myself and set the box of stationery on the counter.

Melinda carried another patty of hamburger over to the griddle and set it down next to hers. "Would you like something to drink?"

"No thank you."

"Coke?"

"Maybe just some water."

She walked to one of the cupboards for a glass, brought it down and held it under a faucet until it was full. Then she carried it over to where I was sitting and set it on the counter. "Thank you," I said. She walked back to the refrigerator and removed a box of rolls to carry to the shelf.

I looked down at my box of stationery, then lifted the lid up and read my name and address printed on the top sheet. "I've got to write this tonight," I said. "I can't put it off any longer."

"Write it now."

"Here?"

She removed two rolls from the box and set them open on the shelf. "Do you have a pen?"

I glanced down at the cash register. "There's a pen down there," I said, "but I guess I'll wait till I'm back at the apartment."

She returned to the refrigerator another time and carried back a small pile of cheese slices.

"The only thing I'm worried about," I said, "is that if it gets too late, sometimes I begin to lose my powers of concentration."

"I know what you mean."

"I'll be writing along and think it's a great letter, then I'll read it over in the morning and see it's just nonsense."

"I know the feeling." She peeled two slices off the pile of cheese and rested one on each piece of meat.

"I've put this letter off so long."

She carried the cheese pile back and put it in the refrigerator.

"I suppose I could explain what happened," I said. "There was a delay in the stationery getting here from the factory."

Melinda removed a head of lettuce from the plastic container and began pulling it apart.

"Let me see something," I said. I leaned forward on the stool and removed a letter from my back pocket. I opened it in front of me. "Let's see. Two weeks. It's been two weeks since the letter was written that I have to answer."

"Did they want an immediate reply?"

"Yes."

Melinda rested some lettuce on two of the roll halves.

"It's this girl," I said, resting the letter on top of the stationery box. "She lives in Wisconsin."

"Is that a fact."

"Beth is her name."

"I don't know her that well, really, but we've been writing back and forth quite a bit."

"Catsup?" Melinda said.

"Here." I held up a catsup dispenser from in front of me on the counter.

She walked over and took it, then glanced down at the letter on the box of stationery. "Is that from Beth?"

"Yes."

"I see she has personal stationery too."

"Yes." I picked it up and ran my finger over the printed name and address at the top. "Hers is in red," I said. "Sort of a script. I guess it's more feminine to have it that way."

"Very effective." Melinda carried the catsup container back to the shelf.

I opened up the letter and read down for the first few lines. "I should have answered this."

"Things pile up."

I read down quickly to the bottom, then turned it over and read down to the signature. "I guess it would be pretty boring to hear anything that it said."

"Feel free."

"The thing is," I said, "it wasn't just a matter of getting the personalized stationery; it's also a matter of not knowing quite what to say to her."

Melinda reached up for a spatula above the griddle.

"Let's see." I turned the letter over to the first part again.

Melinda took the end of the spatula and pried up the edges of one of the patties. "You know what I did," she said. "I put the cheese on top before turning them over." She set the spatula down on the shelf.

"What are you doing."

She took the corner of one of the cheese slices and began trying to peel it up off the meat patty. "You're supposed to put the cheese on after you've flipped them. I forgot." She pulled part of the cheese up off the meat but some of it had melted already and stayed on. She pulled some of the cheese up off the other one, then turned both patties and rested the cheese back down on top of them. "Excuse me," she said. "What were you saying?"

"Nothing," I said. "I was just thinking out loud."

"About what."

"This letter. What I'm going to say in it."

She brought a glass down from the cupboard and held it under the faucet of a Coca-Cola machine against the wall. "What's the problem. What's she demanding of you."

"Nothing. It's just my wording I'm thinking about."

When the glass was filled she removed it from the faucet and took a sip.

"Let me see here." I looked down to about the middle of the first page of the letter. " 'This will be a difficult decision for me to make and I very much hope you will provide me with your counsel.' " I looked up at Melinda.

"What was that," she said.

"That was a sentence from the letter."

She took another sip from the Coca-Cola. "What about it."
"She wants counsel. She's asking me for counsel."
"About what."
I looked back at the letter. "Here's the beginning. 'Dear
Roger. For the past week or so I have been very seriously
debating with myself whether or not to give up the thought
of going all the way for my R.N.' " I looked back up at Me-
linda.
She was looking at me. "What's an R.N."
"A nursing degree."
"Just a minute." She turned around, picked up the spatula
and lifted the edges of the hamburgers. They were sizzling.
She turned down the flame slightly, then turned around
again. "She's thinking of giving up the thought of going all
the way for her nursing degree."
"That's what she says. It's the first time she's said that."
"So what's the next sentence."
I looked back at the letter and found the next sentence.
"Here it is. 'There are, of course, many factors that would
have to be taken into consideration in changing my course.
My parents are a large factor. The fact that my Aunt Nell is
providing half the finances for the tuition is another factor;
she would be very disappointed. Another one is you.' " I
looked back up at Melinda.
"Don't stop."
"Oh." I looked down at the letter again. " 'We know each
other only from that one time. Yet, speaking frankly, I can't
help but feel that with our letters to each other we know each
other as well as we know any other human beings. This may
sound strange to you because we only spent half an hour or
so in each other's company but I don't think it is strange.' " I
gestured at the letter. "Then the sentence about wanting my
counsel."
"Then what."

"What's next?"

"Yes."

"Let's see. 'I realize this is an extremely forward thing for me to propose to you. Yet, on the other hand, I don't feel I can call up Aunt Nell and simply say I've decided to drop out of nursing school on a whim. I could, but it would be a blow to her, with the money she has spent. Instead, what I would like to be able to tell her is that I am leaving school to get married. As I said before, I realize this is forward of me. Yet, I can't help but feel, from the letters we have exchanged over the past year, that we have a world of things in common and common interests. Therefore, I hope very much that your reply will be in the affirmative because there is no doubt in my mind but that we would be extremely happy. Since your work is there I would not feel any regrets about choosing to live in that city, even though I don't know it except for that one day.' " I turned over the letter. "And so on. A line about the weather. Her parents are fine. Her roommate's birthday. 'Love, Beth.' That's it." I folded up the letter and returned it to its envelope.

"You're worried about the wording of your reply," Melinda said.

"I am, yes."

Melinda took another sip from her Coca-Cola. "I can see how you might be." She turned around toward the griddle again.

"I almost always write letters back as soon as I get them. When the letter's fresh in my mind."

Melinda lifted one of the meat patties up off the griddle and rested it on a roll.

"With this one I had the new stationery ordered. I kept putting it off because I wanted to use the new stationery. Now it's very hard to answer it at all."

She put the other patty on the other roll.

"But I have to do it tonight. I'm getting a guilt feeling."

"Do you like catsup?"

"Yes please."

She picked up the catsup dispenser and squirted catsup around on top of each of the meat patties. "What's your answer going to be," she said.

"To Beth?"

She set the dispenser back down on the shelf. "To Beth."

"I'm not sure," I said. "I think I'd better start off by trying to explain why I've waited so long before answering."

Melinda took the tops of the rolls and closed them over the meat patties. She picked one up and carried it over to me.

"Thank you."

"You're welcome." She removed a napkin from the napkin dispenser on the counter and handed it to me.

"Thank you."

"Don't mention it." She turned around and went back to get the other cheeseburger and her glass of Coca-Cola. "You'll start by apologizing for the delay in answering."

"I feel I should."

"And then what." She took a small bite out of the side of her cheeseburger. "What will you say after that."

"Well that's it," I said. I took a bite out of my cheeseburger. "That's it. What will I say after that."

"You don't know."

"I mean I sort of know," I said, "but I don't know quite how to say it."

She took another bite of her cheeseburger and then a sip of the Coke. "What do you sort of think you'll say."

"Let's see if I can word it right."

"Take your time."

I took another bite of the cheeseburger. "This is very good."

"Thank you."

I chewed up the bite and swallowed it. "I think I'll say go ahead and drop out of nursing school. I think that will be the gist of what I'll say."

"And then what." She turned her cheeseburger around and took a bite out of a new side of it.

"Well, I'll say I think I could handle it if she wanted to come out here and go ahead with her idea."

"Of marriage."

"Yes." I cleared my throat, then took a large bite of the cheeseburger.

"You think you could handle it."

"I hope I could."

"Let's see if I've got it right," Melinda said. "First you'll apologize for not writing sooner, explain it was because the personalized stationery didn't come in time; then you'll say you think you could handle it if she wanted to leave school and come out here and marry you. Then you'll sign it and send it."

"Essentially," I said, "but you see it's the wording that's so important."

Melinda turned around and held her glass against the Coke machine till it was filled again. "I assume you haven't been married before."

"Oh no."

"Have there been times you've wished you'd been married?"

I looked down at the surface of the counter. "I can't honestly say there have been times I've wished I was married. I can say there have been times I've gotten a little tired of cooking my own dinners."

"You don't go out."

"I don't like to spend the extra money."

Melinda turned around and set her Coke down and picked

up the spatula again. She began scraping the top of the griddle, pushing the grease off into a little trough at the side. "Do you live in an apartment?"

"Yes."

"By yourself?"

"Yes."

She finished scraping the top of the griddle, then turned on the water in the sink and held the end of the spatula under it. "Will Beth move into your apartment?"

"If she'd like to."

"Why don't you ask her in the letter," Melinda said. "There's another sentence." She turned off the water, shook the spatula and hung it up on its hook over the griddle. "I don't know what else to say. Just congratulations I guess."

"Thank you."

I watched while Melinda carried the plastic container of lettuce back to the refrigerator, set them inside and closed the door. "Let's see," she said. She turned around and looked at the pie rack at the other end of the counter. "Would you care for some pie?"

"No thank you."

"I may." She walked down along the counter to the pie rack, opened its door and looked inside. "Peach."

"Excuse me?"

"Peach or lemon meringue. I think I'll have peach." She reached inside and removed a plate with a piece of peach pie on it. "Fork." She walked to a silverware tray against the wall and removed a fork. Then she cut off the tip of the piece of pie and put it in her mouth.

"How is it."

"Quite good." She cut off another piece, then carried the pie back to the end of the counter and closed the pie rack. "What are your plans," she said.

"Mine?"

"You mentioned calling the police at one point."

"Oh; yes."

"When did you think of doing that." She walked back to the shelf beside the griddle for her Coca-Cola.

"Anytime," I said. "After dinner."

She took a sip of the Coke. "If it's all the same to you," she said, "I'd like to try on a few clothes."

"Where."

"On the second floor. Women's fashions."

"Oh."

She set the Coke down long enough to cut another bite of pie for herself.

"Just go up and put on some clothes?"

"If it's all right."

"Well," I said. I looked down at my stationery box. "I guess if you want to."

"There was a red evening gown up there I'd like to try on if you could spare a minute or two."

"Sure," I said. "I mean I'm free."

"You didn't have a date tonight."

"Oh no."

She came out from behind the counter. "Maybe you could write your letter while I tried on the clothes."

I got down from my stool and reached into my back pocket for my wallet. "Say," I said, "I wish you'd let me pick up the tab for the meal."

"Really?"

"I'd like to."

"That's very kind."

I opened the wallet and removed two dollar bills. "I'll just leave two dollars. It was less than that; about one fifty."

"A generous tip."

"I wonder," I said, returning the wallet to my pocket. "Maybe we should write out a bill so they'll know what we ate."

"Why."

Picking up my stationery box, I said, "I guess it doesn't matter."

"Can you get the light?"

I walked down several stools, reached up and pulled on the string. I could see Melinda's silhouette in the doorway. She started out carrying her Coke, and I followed.

"Tell me," she said, "Why are you a travel agent."

I caught up with her. "Why?"

"Yes."

"I don't know," I said, "I guess I need to make a living."

"But why at that."

We walked up onto the ramp leading to the other part of the store. "I don't know what you mean," I said.

"I mean why not a dry cleaner."

We walked into the other part of the store. "I don't think I'd care for that kind of work."

"You care for being a travel agent though."

"Yes."

"Is it a life's work?"

"I foresee continuing on with it, yes." We walked past an aluminum canoe.

"You're dedicated to it then."

"I plan to go on with it," I said. "It sounds odd to say I'm dedicated to it. It has its rewards."

"What are they."

"Could I ask why you're asking me all this?"

"Because I've never met a travel agent before."

We reached the foot of the escalator and started up. "It would be hard to put into words what the rewards are."

"Reduced travel rates?"

"No."

"What else would they be."

"They're kind of intangible," I said. "Having an office to go to during the day; not having the kind of work where I always feel really rushed."

"You don't work hard then."

"Sometimes."

"But why a travel agent." She stopped, turned around and looked down at me.

"It's hard to put into words," I said. "A customer comes in. We talk awhile, then he leaves. A new person comes, and goes. That's a kind of reward." I gestured toward the top. "We'd better go up."

"He comes in," she said, "he goes out, and you feel rewarded."

"Right."

She shrugged and continued up.

"My brother's been married six times," Melinda said as we reached the top. "It's too bad he isn't here to give you some advice about your letter." We walked past a jewelry counter, then came into a section of women's clothes. Melinda stopped in front of a mannequin wearing a long red gown. "That's the one I saw."

"The gown."

"Yes." She looked at it, then walked slowly around it.

"Did you think of removing it from the dummy?" I said.

"If I can't find another." She started over toward a clothes rack. When she got to it she set her Coke down on the carpet and started going through dresses hanging on the rack. "Why don't you use the counter," she pointed over at a sales counter, "to write your letter on."

I walked over to the counter. "I may do that."

"Do you need a pen? There may be one in my purse."

"I have one." I reached into my inside coat pocket for a pen, then set the box of stationery down on the counter and removed its lid.

"Do you make first drafts of letters?"

"Not usually."

"It would be a waste to do it on personalized stationery." She continued going through the dresses on the rack.

I set the box of stationery in its lid and unscrewed the top of the pen.

"I like this one," Melinda said. "Do you like this one?" She was holding out the sleeve of a white dress.

"Right."

"I like it." She removed its hanger from the rack. "Do you see a changing room?"

"Over there I think."

"Oh yes." She walked past me and pulled aside a curtain, then walked in and let it close behind her.

I wrote the date at the top of the page.

"If you need any help with wording," Melinda said, "let me know."

"I'm just going to say I would have written sooner except that the stationery didn't get here till today." There was some rustling of cloth on the other side of the curtain. I wrote "Dear Beth," at the top of the page. Then I wrote, "There is really no excuse I can make for going so long without replying to your letter. The only reason I can give is that I ordered some personalized stationery and wanted to wait for it so I could use it to write you on." I stopped writing and read it over.

"How did you happen to meet this girl?" Melinda said from the other side of the curtain.

"Beth?"

"She said in her letter she was here for just a day."

"She was," I said. "Last summer." I went back and made a darker dot on the *i* in the word *write*. "There was a bus tour. Some nursing students from Wisconsin organized a tour of New England. When they got here they worked through our agency. I arranged a historical bus tour through Boston for them."

"Oh?"

"A three-hour trip around the historical sights."

"Were you the guide?"

"For the walking part I was — then the rest on a chartered bus. Beth was sort of the spokesman for the group. That's how I happened to be talking to her the most."

"I guess one thing led to another with the two of you."

"Sort of. They came back at the end of the tour and thanked me. About two weeks later Beth wrote from Wisconsin that she had lost one of her gloves on the trip and wondered if she might have left it in the travel agency."

"Oh?"

"She hadn't. I looked around, but she hadn't. I wrote back saying I couldn't find it. Then about a week later she wrote again, thanking me for writing and saying she enjoyed the historical points. She also said school was sort of a grind and if I felt like dropping her a letter, just about the weather or whatever I wanted, it would make things pleasant for her."

There was more rustling on the other side of the curtain. "So you did."

"I did, yes."

"And she wrote back."

"She wrote back all about her family. Her aunt and so forth. As you said, one thing led to another." I looked back down at the letter. "I'd better write this." I lowered the pen to the page again, waited a moment, then wrote, "Do you like the new stationery? I hope you do." I reread what I had written. "It's kind of hard to write standing up like this."

"You need a desk."

"I mean I guess I can do it this way. It's just that I'm not used to writing standing up."

"How's the letter going?"

"I'm just telling her about the stationery." I looked back at the page and tried to think of a way to begin a new paragraph. It was a minute or so later and I was still trying to think of how to start the next paragraph when Melinda came out from between the curtains. She had taken off her shoes and was wearing the white gown. "How does it look," she said.

"Good."

She walked to a three-way mirror, stopped, turned and looked at her reflection over her shoulder. "It's some kind of silk," she said. She turned around the other way to see herself over the other shoulder.

I looked down at my page.

"What have you said so far."

"You can read it."

She walked over beside me, leaned forward and read what I had written. "Now what," she said.

"That's what I'm trying to decide."

She walked over to pick up her Coke. "Why don't you tell her where you are?"

"Now?"

"Tell her you're locked in a store with a girl."

I looked down at the rug. "I don't think I will."

"You don't consider it newsworthy."

"It's newsworthy, but she might . . . I just don't think I'll mention it."

Melinda took a sip of her Coke and walked back to the mirror.

"No offense," I said.

"Oh no."

"I mean I'm sure this is something I'll mention to her in the future. I'll tell her about it."

Melinda turned to the side and held the white material in against herself. "Look back on it."

"Sure."

"You'll reminisce about it with Beth."

She walked past the end of a counter, set the Coke down and reached up to remove a hat from the head of a mannequin. "You just don't want to mention it now."

"I'd like to wait."

She fixed the hat on her head and walked back to the mirror. "Why," she said. She tilted it slightly.

"Excuse me?"

"God what a nightmare." She removed the hat and carried it back to the dummy's head. Behind the counter was another hat, a white one with a blue feather sticking up from it. Melinda went behind the counter, picked it up and put it on her head. "Why do you feel squeamish about mentioning it."

"I wouldn't say I felt squeamish."

She walked to the mirror and tilted her head.

"I'd say I had other reasons for writing the letter. Specific things I have to say."

"I thought it was your custom to exchange bits of news with her." She turned the hat around so the feather was sticking out toward the back.

"It is."

She smoothed the feather. "Don't worry," she said, "you're not the first one not to consider me newsworthy." She picked up her Coke and started along the counter. In the center of it was a form of a head with several strings of beads and pearls around it. She removed them and fitted them around the hat and around her neck. "Have you noticed my accent?"

"What's that."

"I have a southern accent," she said. "Quite a few people have commented on it since I've been here. I thought maybe you didn't notice it."

"Oh I did."

She started back. "But you didn't comment on it or feel like asking me where I was from."

"I've heard them before."

She nodded.

"But I did notice it."

"I wasn't sure," she said. "Most people up here ask me where I'm from." She took a sip of the Coke. "I noticed you didn't ask me where I was from."

"Where."

"I mean I don't want to force information on you. It's just that most people like to get acquainted with each other. I've noticed you don't seem to do this."

I looked down at my letter.

"The small formalities," she said, "I've never known anyone to neglect them like you do." She walked back to the mirror to look at the beads and pearls around her neck.

"What small formalities."

She smoothed the pearls over her breasts. "The things that people talk about. You don't seem to like to talk about them."

"Like where you come from?"

"That's one of them."

I looked down at my letter for a moment, then back at Melinda. "I'd like to know."

"It's all right."

"I would."

She turned to the side and draped some of the beads over one of her shoulders. "You don't have to pretend. If you're not interested in me, you're not interested in me." She shrugged the shoulder with beads over it.

"Are you from the South?"

"Right."

"I'd like to know where you're from," I said. "I'm not usually rude, I usually observe the formalities."

She walked over to her purse and slipped her arm through the strap. "I don't want to interfere with the letter."

"I'd like to know about you," I said. "Really."

"What would you like to know."

"Your family?" I said. "Your parents?"

"I had three fathers," she said. "The longest one I had was from age eight to age seventeen. There was one before that, then one afterwards."

"One mother."

"Yes. One older brother. One older sister."

It was quiet for a few moments.

"Anything you'd like to say," I said, "I'd like to hear. Is your mother happy with your third father?"

"She says she is. He imports rubber. I could have had a job with him as a secretary but I couldn't accept working for my stepfather." She walked over to the foot of the escalator and rested her hand on the railing.

"Did your mother want you to come up here?"

"No."

"She let you come though."

"She said I was ungrateful. She said I wouldn't like it up here. She said I'd be back, but she let me come."

"Did you . . ."

"I don't like it down there either," she said. "Everywhere seems kind of boring to me. It always has."

"You feel bored now?"

"Depressed."

"You don't act like you're depressed."

"Not depressed. Just . . . I couldn't say. There's no word really for it. My mother isn't up here; I suppose that makes it a little better."

"You didn't ever like her?"

"She was an actress," Melinda said. "She wanted us all to go into the theater. None of us wanted to, so it was always kind of uncomfortable in the house."

"She was a famous actress?"

"She just did local things." Melinda looked down at a stair of the escalator. "She drinks quite a lot now. That's the main reason I finally left. My fathers spent their time trying to stop her from drinking. One would give up, then the next one would start in. I could have told them even before they married her what she wanted them for."

"Which was what."

"Just to have someone around to tell her to stop drinking. It would have been a bore for her to drink if there was no one there to tell her not to. I used to tell her all the time she was ruining herself with liquor. Then I realized that must be what she wanted to do and stopped telling her."

"Does your mother still act?"

"Sometimes the chamber of commerce sobers her up for a Christmas pageant. She hasn't done any serious things for quite a while. She'd much rather have people come over to the house and tell her she's a tragic actress, doomed, out of her time."

"You never tried to act yourself."

"She forced me to go to acting school till I was twelve. Then I started hiding every Tuesday afternoon when it was time to go. Finally she gave up."

"And you don't feel at all like helping her."

"She doesn't want to be helped — that's what I finally came to see." Melinda started slowly up the escalator.

"Are you going up?"

"I thought I would." She climbed on up toward the top, then stopped and turned around. "Could you do something for me?" she said.

"What is it."

"When they come to let you out, can you tell them you're the only one in the store?"

"What for."

She didn't answer, but started walking up the escalator, carrying her Coke.

I went partway toward the escalator, then stopped. "Melinda?" I watched the back of the white dress as she ascended the rest of the way then disappeared. I waited a moment longer, then walked back to the letter. I picked up the pen again and reread what I had written. Just as I was about to start a new sentence I thought I heard a noise and looked up. It sounded as though she had started coming back down the escalator but she hadn't. I continued looking off at the escalator a few moments, then back at the letter. "Concerning your plan of leaving nursing school," I wrote, "although you didn't go into any specific reasons for wanting to take this step, I'm sure you had reasons, and that you are aware of the best thing to do. As I've said before, I hope you will come to Boston and we'll be able to spend more time together. As far as your idea of getting married is concerned, though I guess I should tell you it comes as something of a surprise, yet, after the first shock, I can't honestly say that I don't feel that there might be some chance of working something out along these lines after discussing it and seeing what we felt the situation to be." I looked back over what I had written. "Too wordy," I said. Again I looked

up at the escalator. "Melinda?" There was no answer. After
a few moments more I then picked up the top to my pen,
screwed it on and returned the pen to my pocket. I put the
lid on the box of stationery, then walked over to the curtain
in front of the dressing room. I pulled it open. The skirt and
sweater Melinda had been wearing were draped over the
back of a chair and her shoes were on the chair's seat. I
looked at them a moment, then reached in and picked them
up. I turned around and carried them between the aisles of
counters and toward the escalator; then I started up.

When I got to the top I stopped and looked from the table
settings to the beds to the racks of dresses, but I didn't see
her. "Hello?" I waited for her to answer then walked over
and saw her.

She was at the other side of the floor, still wearing the
dress and the hat, with two sheets and a blanket over one of
her arms. Under her other arm was a pillow. I watched as
she walked to the bed where I had carried her after she
fainted. She pulled the bedspread off, then shook one of the
sheets over the mattress, smoothed it down, then the next.
She smoothed the second one down, and began walking
around the bed tucking them in. I walked past several dining room tables until I was standing a bed away from her.

"Did you finish the letter?" She tucked the sheets in at the
bottom.

"I think I'll rewrite it."

She moved around to the other side. "I got the sheets and
blanket over in the linen department." She bent over and
picked up the blanket from the floor, shook it out and let it
fall across the bed. "I thought I'd need this. It's fairly warm
now, but it might get chilly later on." She walked along the
side of the bed tucking the blanket in under the mattress.

"I brought these." I held out her skirt, sweater and shoes.

"Can you set them on a chair?"

I walked to a small easy chair at the end of the bed and draped the skirt and sweater over its back and set the shoes on its seat. Melinda tucked the blanket in along the bottom of the bed. Then she picked up the bedspread and pulled it up over the blanket. The pillow was resting on the floor at my feet. I picked it up and handed it to her. "Thank you." She set it at the head of the bed, then stood and looked around. She walked past several beds and to a small table. On it was a small white clock. She picked it up, looked at the back of it, then started winding it up as she walked back toward the bed. "What time do you have."

I looked at my watch. "Just quarter of eight."

She turned one of the knobs on the back of the clock, then walked over to seat herself on the edge of the bed. "What time do they open here."

"I don't know," I said. "Nine?"

"I'll set it for seven." She turned another knob on the back of the clock, then set it on the floor beside the bed. "I've been job-hunting all day," she said. "Maybe I'll turn in even though it's early." She reached behind her back, bending forward slightly, until she found the tab of the zipper at the top of her dress. She pulled it partway down from her neck with one hand, then changed her position slightly and pulled it the rest of the way down with her other hand.

"You're going to bed here?"

She stood up and let the dress fall down around her feet, then stepped out of it, bent over to pick it up and carried it to a chair. She folded it in half and rested it over the back of the chair. Then she removed the hat and set it on top of the dress. After that she removed the strings of beads and pearls and coiled them up on top of the hat. She turned around and walked back to the bed, turned down the covers and got in.

Then she rested on her elbow a moment looking off at one of the lamps. "I guess I'll leave the lights on. It seems like too much trouble to turn them all off." She moved down in the bed and put her head on the pillow, then pulled the sheet up till it came to just under her ear. "Good night," she said.

For several minutes she lay quietly while I stood looking at her and holding the stationery box under my arm.

"Melinda?" I said finally.

"I don't know if I can sleep with the lamps on or not," she said. "I'm used to pitch dark at night."

I walked over to the bed, looked down at her a moment, then seated myself beside her. "Melinda?" She didn't answer. I set the stationery box down on the floor. She moved down slightly farther under the covers. I was sitting so that the form of her shoulder was very close to my hip. I moved my hand over, held it above her shoulder for a moment, then rested it on her shoulder.

"That feels nice," she said, not turning over.

"It does?"

She nodded.

I continued sitting beside her with my hand on her shoulder. I looked down at her black hair and at her cheek. Finally her shoulder moved and she turned over onto her back and looked up at me. She brought one of her hands up out of the covers to push some hair out of one of her eyes. Then she reached up and rested her hand on the side of my face. She smiled at me. After a few moments more I moved my head down slowly until it came close to hers and then I rested my lips very softly against hers. We stayed like that without moving. "Can you get in the bed?" she said.

"Yes." I pulled back the covers.

"Can you leave your clothes outside the bed?"

I bent over and untied my shoes and pulled them off, then

I pulled off my socks. I stood and unbuckled my belt, then turned so that I was facing away from the bed and pushed my pants and shorts down along my legs. "I'm sorry I didn't seem more interested in you."

"It's all right."

I stepped out of my pants. "I'm sorry I didn't ask where you were from."

"I'm from Charleston."

"South Carolina?"

"It doesn't matter." I felt her hand on one of my legs.

I quickly pulled my tie out from under my shirt collar and dropped it on my pants. "It's not that I wasn't interested," I said, "but I didn't know how to act at first." I removed my arms from the sleeves of my coat, then dropped the coat on the floor. "I was interested right from the first."

She moved her hand up and down along the side of my leg.

"You're beautiful," I said, unbuttoning my shirt quickly. "I was shy because you were beautiful." I finished unbuttoning my shirt and dropped it on the floor. Then I turned around and pulled up the covers and got quickly into the bed. She had removed her bra and panties. "Really. That's why I was shy."

"All right."

"With this Beth person writing me asking me to marry her you must think the girls are after me, that I have lots of girls."

She reached up and pushed her fingers into the hair at the side of my head. "Shhh," she said.

"It's not true though."

She moved my head slowly down toward hers.

"I mean I was nervous. I didn't know what to say to you."

"Okay," she said.

"It's not that I wasn't interested in you from the very first."

"Can you kiss me?" She brought my head down closer to hers.

"Just this one thing," I said, turning my face to the side. "Right from the first moment you came falling down the stairs I thought to myself you were one of the most beautiful girls I had ever seen."

She moved her head up and put her lips against my cheek.

"But I didn't know how to act with you. That's why you got the impression I wasn't interested in you; but I can tell you it's the farthest thing from the truth." I felt her hand moving down my side under the covers and along my leg. "It is." I felt her pushing herself underneath me. "What if a watchman comes."

She moved her face around to kiss my lips. "There's no watchman."

"What if he comes up from the basement."

"There's no basement."

I could feel her opening her legs and then wrapping them around me under the covers. "I hope you're right."

"Shhh."

"I feel I should be honest and say that I'm very nervous right now."

"Stop talking." I felt her hand moving between my legs.

"I can't seem to."

"Try."

"I am."

"Try harder."

She pushed her lips, which were wet, up against mine and opened her mouth.

2

ROGER HART
48 BEACON STREET
BOSTON, MASSACHUSETTS 02108

May 10

DEAR BETH,

Thank you for your letter, which arrived two weeks ago.

Firstly, I apologize for taking so long to write back. I feel badly about this and have no very good excuse except that I was anxious to write you on some new stationery I had ordered (see letterhead above) and kept waiting for it to come before writing. It finally came in yesterday and I am now writing.

I'm glad to hear you're well and that your parents are fine also. Please give a belated birthday greeting to Joanne from me.

It is just before nine here and I am writing this at my desk in the travel agency. Mr. Becker is still on vacation with his family and I am holding things down. It is getting rather hectic, I must confess, with the spring tourist season now in full swing, and I will be most happy when he returns next week.

I am trying to think of news but there really isn't that much. Work is heavy during the day and the nights are also taken up with work, making up ticket forms and other exciting things like this. Itineraries etc.

It is just nine so I had better close. I will not neglect our

correspondence as I have been lately, however, and you
can expect to hear from me again soon.

Love,
ROGER

P.S. What about the Spring Festival the nursing school was
putting on and in which you were one of the organizers? This
sounded very interesting. You mentioned it letter-before-last,
then didn't mention it again last letter. Did it come off okay?
Please give me a rundown on this as it sounded very interesting.

R.

I removed an envelope from the stationery box, addressed
it, folded the letter in three and inserted it into the envelope.
There was a booklet of airmail stamps in my desk drawer. I
tore one out and returned the booklet to the drawer. I licked
the stamp and placed it on the corner of the envelope, licked
the flap and sealed it, then pushed the swivel chair back and
stood.

The door of the office had a sign stuck on it by a suction
cup. It said OPEN on one side and CLOSED on the other. I
turned the sign around and stuck the suction cup back on
the glass so that the OPEN side faced out to the street. Then
I unlocked the door and stepped outside. I walked down to
the corner where there was a mailbox, opened it and
dropped the letter inside. The large Statler Hilton Hotel was
down about half a block and on the other side of the street. I
stood a few moments looking at it, then turned around and
walked back along the sidewalk and into the travel agency
again.

It was the quietest morning I had had for a long time.
For the first two hours nobody came in or called. I spent the
morning typing up an itinerary. First I set the tickets and

reservations out on the blotter, then went down the list, place by place and date by date. It was a six-week tour of the British Isles. They had planned to stay a night in each place only, so it was a long one with many hotels on it and covered three pages. When I was done I typed "Happy Traveling — drop us a card if you think of it," then removed the page from the typewriter, assembled all four copies that I had made and went through them quickly, checking the reservation slips and ticket slips on the desk to be sure I had made no error. When I had done that I opened the drawer again and brought out a stapler. I stapled the corner of each copy of the itinerary, then removed an envelope from the drawer, folded the itinerary and put it inside. I wrote the people's name on the front of the envelope and put the envelope in the desk. I got up with the carbon copy and carried it across the room to a gray filing cabinet, then walked back to my desk.

It was close to ten o'clock and the next thing I did was to call the employment agency to find a job for Melinda. The man I knew there was named Dupres.

"Mr. Dupres," I said when he answered, "I'm Roger Hart over at the travel agency. You booked through me a year ago on your Rocky Mountain spring tour."

"Oh yes."

"I'm calling," I said, "because a friend of mine needs a job. She just got into town and I wondered if I could send her over to talk to you."

"By all means," Mr. Dupres said.

"Melinda Gray's her name," I said, "I'll send her over."

"I'll be looking for her."

At ten-fifteen Melinda still hadn't come in. I pulled the phone book across the desk, opened it and found the number for the Statler Hilton. Then I pulled the phone toward me and rested my hand on the receiver. I decided I would wait till just ten-twenty and if she hadn't come in I would call then. I waited in the chair with my hand resting on the phone for four minutes and was just about to pick it up and dial when a man came through the door, looked around, then stepped up in front of a colored poster of one of the Swiss Alps that was on the wall. "Good morning," I said.

"Oh," he said, turning around, "I thought you were phoning."

"May I help you?"

He stepped up to the other side of the desk. "I wondered if you had a brochure of the Bahamas."

I pushed my chair back and walked across the room to the filing cabinet again. I pulled open the top drawer and parted the papers at B. I removed several colored brochures. "How are these," I said.

The man was at another wall examining a large poster depicting a volcano in Japan. He turned around. "Oh yes." He took them. "Oh yes." He looked at the front of each one. "Yes."

"Are you planning a trip there?"

"I may be." He put the brochures into his inside coat pocket. "I'm not sure yet."

We were standing next to the front table. There was a cardboard replica of the Eiffel Tower in the center of the table with a cardboard French flag coming out of the top of it. The man picked it up a moment and looked at it, then set it down.

"When might you want to go," I said.

"I'm just not sure yet," he said. "I'm really not definite yet."

I turned around and walked back to the other side of the desk. "Why don't we do this," I said. "If you can give me your name and phone number we can get together when things start to get more definite."

"It's Montgomery."

I removed a sheet of paper from a scratch pad at the side of the desk and picked up a pen.

"I don't have a phone right now," he said. He was over at another wall looking at a rack of airplane schedules.

"Will you be getting one soon?"

"I may be. Yes, I will be."

I put the sheet of paper at the edge of the desk. "Why don't you call me and let me know what it is when you get it."

"I will." He patted at the outside of the breast pocket where he had put the brochures. "And thank you for these."

"Don't mention it."

He walked out the door. I watched him walk along the sidewalk past the front window and out of sight, then looked at the phone again and picked up the receiver. I dialed the number of the Statler Hilton Hotel. The telephone was answered almost the moment it buzzed. "Statler Hilton," a girl said.

"I believe you have a Miss Melinda Gray staying there."

There was a silence of a few moments. "May I ring her for you?"

"Yes."

There was a click and then a buzzing noise. Another click. "Her phone is in use, sir."

"Thank you, I'll call again." I hung up.

I waited five minutes before calling again. While I was waiting I straightened the blotter on the desk, rested the telephone directly in the center of the blotter and neatened the telephone book and the memo pad at the other edge of the desk. There was an electric clock on one corner of the desk.

I turned it slightly till it was facing me more directly and then when it read just ten-thirty I picked up the receiver of the telephone again and dialed the Statler Hilton. "Melinda Gray's room please."

"One moment."

This time the phone rang. There were two and a half rings before she answered. "Yes?"

"Melinda," I said. "How did you make out."

There was a silence. "Who is this."

"Me."

There was another silence.

"It's Roger," I said.

Another silence.

"Roger Hart?"

"Oh."

I waited for her to say something more but she didn't. "I wondered how you made out," I said finally. "You went in the ladies' room." There was a long, long silence. I moved the receiver around to my other ear. "After we got up this morning. At the store. You went in the ladies' room to wait for them to open and I went into the men's room. I waited about an hour in there. Then I just went out and downstairs and came here to work. I didn't see you."

I heard a muffled voice on the other end, then silence for a moment, then the muffled voice again. Then she spoke into the phone again. "Hello?" she said.

"What's happening."

"Everything's fine," she said.

"You got out all right."

"Yes."

I looked down at the blotter. "I just wondered about the job appointment," I said. "I called a friend of mine at an employment agency."

Again there was the sound of a muffled voice at the other end.

"Melinda?"

"I'm sorry," she said. "You called a friend."

"Is someone else there?" I said.

"They're just taking my breakfast dishes away."

"Oh." I returned the receiver to the original ear. "Here's the situation. There's a Mr. Dupres at an employment agency who's looking for you."

"Roger?" she said. "Can I call you back?"

"What for."

"I'll call you back in about half an hour," she said. "Thank you. Goodbye." There was a click.

I waited a few moments, holding the phone up to my ear and looking down at the blotter, then there was another click. "Good morning," a girl said, "Statler Hilton." I lowered the receiver back to the telephone.

A Mr. John Bell came into the office a little later to pick up a plane ticket for Lima for himself and his wife. I was still seated at the desk when he came through the door. "Yes?" I said, getting up, "may I help you?"

He walked up to the desk. "I've come for a plane reservation," he said.

"Please sit down," I gestured at a chair on the other side of the desk. He sat down in it, then I sat down in my chair again. "Now," I said, "where is it you'd like to go." I reached over for the pad of paper and my pen. "First, let me get your name here." I looked up at him. He was holding his hat in his lap and looking over the desktop at me. "I'm Roger Hart," I said, "why don't I get your name down for a start."

"We've been through all this," he said.

"Excuse me?"

"Yesterday we went all through this. I just came in to pick up the ticket."

"Oh." I pushed the paper and pen to the side of the desk again. "I'm sorry." I stood up. "You're Mr. Peters."

"Mr. Bell."

"Bell." I snapped my fingers. "The ticket." I walked over to the filing cabinet against the wall and pulled open the bottom drawer. "Sorry," I said, running my finger past the A section and separating the papers at the B section. "Here." I removed a small folder with his name and his wife's name on the front of it and turned around. "I hope there's nothing wrong with it."

"With what," he said, taking it.

"I mean I'm sure it's all in order. I'm sure you'll enjoy the trip." I looked at him a moment, then held out my hand. "Enjoy the trip."

He shook my hand. "Thank you."

"Good, I'm sure you will."

I sat in the chair, holding a pen and rolling it back and forth between my fingers. Sometimes I looked out the door at the cars, sometimes at the paper Eiffel Tower on the table and sometimes just at the dust in a beam of sunshine falling across the corner of my desk. There were no phone calls for the rest of the morning.

There's a coffee shop on the corner of the block where the travel agency is. Since Mr. Becker had been gone I had gotten in the habit of calling down to the coffee shop and asking them to make me up a sandwich and a cup of milk, then ten minutes later gone down to pick it up and carry it back to eat at my desk. This was so I wouldn't miss any customers that might have come in during the lunch hour. When Mr. Becker was working with me I usually went out to eat first, then came back in forty-five minutes so that he could go out.

At eleven-thirty I thought about calling the hotel again, then decided not to. About twenty minutes before twelve I got up from the chair and walked out the front door. Partway down the block I could see a woman who had been in yesterday to order a ticket. She was in her car, maneuvering into a parking space against the curb. I quickly inserted my key into the lock on the door and turned it, tested the doorknob to be sure it was locked, then walked down the sidewalk in the opposite direction from the woman. At the corner I crossed the street and started back the other way, toward the hotel. I looked over the traffic at the woman as she walked up to the front door of the travel agency and tried the door, then as she bent forward and held her hands beside her eyes and peered in through the glass door.

I walked past some shops in the front of the hotel, then pushed through the glass door and into the lobby. I walked past some chairs where people sat with their luggage and up to the desk. "Which room is Melinda Gray staying in please."

Behind the counter a man had a handful of letters which he was sorting into boxes. He sorted a few more, then stepped to the side and looked up on a chart on the wall. "Room six hundred eight," he said.

"Thank you."

I walked to a row of elevators against the wall, then noticed the stairs beside them and walked up the stairs instead. There was a thick maroon carpet covering the stairs and covering the floor of the hallway on the sixth floor. I walked across it as the numbers on the doors went down through the fifties and through the forties, then there was a hallway. I made a right turn and started down the hall, reading the numbers on the doors as they went down through the twenties. A maid came out of a room pushing a cart. I walked on past her, then stopped. 608 was the next room.

The door was slightly ajar. From where I was standing I couldn't see into the whole room but only part of another

door inside. There was no noise inside the room. I rested
my hand on the knob. The wheels of the cart squeaked as
the maid wheeled it over the carpet behind me. I pushed the
door in a few more inches and bent my head forward so I
could see into part of the room with one eye.

In the corner was the edge of a window with a curtain
over it and a radiator against the wall. Then a floor lamp,
and beside the floor lamp was an easy chair. Seated in the
easy chair, reading a magazine, was a man. He had black
hair and a short beard, and was slouched down in the chair
with his legs straight out in front, crossed at the ankles. I
could only see half of him because of the angle of the door. I
didn't open it farther. He was wearing a red-and-yellow
striped vest and holding the magazine up in front of him,
turning the pages. There was a cigarette in his mouth and to
the side so I couldn't see him for a moment, then he eased
himself back into the chair without the cigarette. There was
no noise in the room except for the rustling of the paper as
he turned the pages.

I turned and looked down the hall. The maid's cart was
just outside the next door down. She stepped out a moment,
glanced at me, then took a rag from the top of her cart and
went back into the room. I looked at the door back into 608.
The man in the chair turned another page. I heard running
water, then the sound of the water stopped. It was quiet for
a few moments, then I heard a new sound which was a
scratching sound. I glanced up and through the crack again
to see the man holding a match at the end of a cigarette between his lips. When it was lit he shook out the match, put
it somewhere on the other side of the chair, then picked the
magazine up from his lap again and held it in front of his
face.

Finally what I decided to do was to open the door wider. I

reached out and put my finger against the wood, waited a moment, then pushed. It opened several more inches. There was no sound. By looking in I could see the entire chair and the man sitting in it. There was a small table beside the chair, and on the table an ashtray with several cigarette butts in it. I raised my hand, put my finger against the wood again and pushed it farther open. The man still didn't look up. As I pushed the door farther, the edge of a bed came into view. On it was an open suitcase. I could just see one corner of it, so I pushed the door farther till I could see the rest of it. It had two sweaters packed in one side of it. A pair of nylon stockings were resting across the suitcase and beside them on the bed was a pair of black low-heeled shoes. I pushed the door open slightly farther, and the man looked up.

I stood in the doorway, my arm out to the side and my finger resting on the door. He lowered his magazine about two inches and looked over the top of it. A line of smoke rose up at the side of his face and into the air. He looked at me for a few moments, then raised the magazine up over his eyes again. Then he turned to a new page.

I lowered my arm from the door. There was the sound of running water again, coming from the other side of a closed door beyond the bed, then the sound stopped. I took a step into the room, then cleared my throat. The man behind the magazine didn't look up. I studied the picture on the front of the magazine for a few moments, then took another step into the room. Without looking up, he removed the cigarette from his mouth and moved it over the ashtray, tapped it once so that its ash fell into the tray, then returned it to his lips and took up the side of the magazine that had sagged down when he had let go of it. After a few more moments he turned another page. "Excuse me," I said.

He lowered the magazine but didn't say anything.

"I was told downstairs that this was Melinda Gray's room."

He sat looking at me over the top of the magazine.

"Is it?" I said.

He nodded, just once, then the magazine went up and covered his eyes again.

I looked over at the closed door in the corner. "Is she in there?"

He didn't answer.

"Excuse me."

The magazine came down again.

"Is Melinda in there?"

He waited another moment, then called, without removing the cigarette from his mouth and without looking away from me. "Melinda!"

She called back from the other side of the door. "What is it."

"Somebody's here."

It was quiet for a few moments. I took another step forward and the man continued looking at me over the magazine.

"Who is it," Melinda called.

"It's me," I said. "Roger."

There was no answer. The man looked back down at the magazine. I took another step into the room, then stopped again. "Melinda?"

There was another pause. "I'm drying my hair," she said finally.

The man's feet were stretched out in front of him and the tips of his shoes were about an inch away from the wheel at the corner of the bed. "Excuse me," I said. I stepped over his ankles and walked to the bathroom door. "Melinda?"

"I'll be out later."

I put my hand on the doorknob, then turned it. "I'd like to come in," I said, "if I could." I opened the door and pushed it several inches in. Melinda was standing in front of the sink, rubbing her hair with a towel. She was wearing a blue bathrobe. "I don't have that much time," I said, stepping partway through the door. "I'm just on my lunch hour."

"Could you close the door? It's freezing."

I stepped all the way into the bathroom and closed the door. Melinda continued to rub her hair with the towel. "I'm sorry I didn't get over at ten," she said. "Did you call up someone?"

"Mr. Dupres."

She leaned slightly forward over the sink and rubbed at the right side of her head. "I should have called you," she said. "I'm sorry I didn't."

"You got out of the store all right," I said.

"I just waited till nine or so. Then I just walked out of the ladies' room and down the stairs and out the door." She swung her hair around to the other side of her head and began rubbing it some more.

"I guess they won't have any way of finding out who it was," I said. "When they find the sheets and blankets and everything under the bed I guess there'll be no way of tracing it."

"I don't see how."

She tossed her damp hair over the top of her head and draped the towel around her neck. Then she reached out and rubbed a large circle in the steam on a mirror over the sink.

"That fellow in the next room," I said.

She removed the towel from her neck and began wiping it across the front of the mirror till it was all cleared.

"The fellow in the chair?"

"Sal."

She dropped the towel on the floor. Then she picked up a comb from the sink and began running it back through her hair.

"Sal," I said.

"That's his name. Sal Hobbes."

I glanced at the door. "He didn't say anything. At first I thought I had the wrong room."

"He's quiet."

"Yes." I looked back at Melinda as she continued to run the comb down through her hair.

"Would you believe my hair used to go down to my waist?"

"No."

She stopped combing for a moment and looked around. "Could you hand me those tissues?"

"What's that."

She pointed to a box of Kleenex resting on the back of the toilet. I walked over and picked them up and handed them to her. She removed one and handed the box back. I returned it to the back of the toilet. She took the sheet of Kleenex, straightened it out and pasted it across her forehead. "You ought to do that," she said.

"What's that."

"I noticed your forehead's sweating too. It's the humidity in here from the steam." She began combing her hair again. The sheet of white Kleenex clung to her forehead.

"I guess I won't."

"It's good to sweat," she said, "but I hate getting it in my eyes."

I watched her combing her hair a few more moments, then lowered the toilet seat and sat down. "I shouldn't really be away from the agency," I said.

"I thought it was your lunch hour."

"I should really eat my lunch in the agency while Mr. Becker's away."

She bent sideways slightly and began combing the hair down at the side of her head.

"I just wanted to get things straightened out," I said, "that's the thing."

She turned on one of the faucets of the sink, ran the comb under it, then began combing her hair again. "You really should put a Kleenex on your forehead," she said. "I can see the sweat running all into your eyes."

I twisted around and picked up the box of Kleenex and removed one sheet. Then I put the box back on the back of the toilet seat, straightened out the sheet and pressed it against my forehead. I removed my hand and it stayed, stuck to the skin. "This Sal," I said, "is he from Boston?"

"He's from New York. I met him on the bus coming up from Charleston."

I could feel one corner of the Kleenex starting to peel away from my forehead. I pressed it back. "A New Yorker."

"Let me show you a trick." Melinda reached out and pinched the two top corners of the Kleenex. "That makes it stay on better."

"Thank you."

She went back to combing her hair. "He's in advertising," she said. "He has an agency down in New York."

I reached up again to press on the Kleenex. "Right offhand I didn't think he was in advertising."

Melinda opened the door of the medicine cabinet and removed a small red plastic box.

"Do you know the name of his firm?"

"Hobbes I think." She opened the top of the small box. Inside was a small black brush and some mascara. "It's just a small one." She rubbed the bristles of the brush back and forth in the mascara. "He's the founder." She leaned toward the mirror and began stroking her eyelashes. "He's expanding," Melinda said. "That's why he needs a new secretary." She blinked, then turned the brush the other way and began brushing the top of the eyelash.

The right side of the Kleenex slid down across my eye. "A new secretary," I said. I pushed it back up.

"That's the reason, yes."

I held the side of the Kleenex up against my forehead and watched her as she leaned forward even farther and inspected the eyelash. "The reason for what."

"This damn stuff is drying up." She put her brush back down in the mascara and began rubbing it around again.

"The reason for what," I said. I got up from the toilet seat. "You aren't . . . you wouldn't be going down to New York with him."

Melinda leaned forward again and began brushing at the eyelash. In the mirror I could look into the reflection of the opening at the top of her bathrobe and see the reflection of one of her breasts.

"Melinda?"

"All that rush this morning: the confusion of getting the sheets hidden, getting into the bathroom, all that, there were some things I didn't get a chance to tell you." She rubbed the brush again in the mascara. "I think there might have been a false impression," she said, "that's the thing I was worried about, that I might have created a false impression last night in the store." She leaned up to the mirror and began brushing the other eyelash.

"You're going to New York?"

"He needs a secretary, yes."

I removed the sopping piece of Kleenex from my forehead. "I haven't seen him since the bus trip up from Charleston.

He came to the hotel this morning. He just said he remembered me and remembered I told him I was going to stay at the Statler and came up to see if I wanted to be his secretary."

I crumpled up the Kleenex and dropped it in a wastebasket beside the sink. "Let's think a minute."

"As you know, I've been having trouble finding work in Boston."

"Till now." I turned around and pulled up another sheet of Kleenex from the Kleenex box and put it on my forehead. "Till now you've been having trouble because you haven't had the right connections."

"This isn't my town."

"Don't be too sure." I walked around to the side of her. "Listen, this Dupres. Mr. Dupres over at the employment agency. Get dressed and go on over there. See what he has for you." Melinda blinked both her eyes, then moved her head several inches backward to look at her reflection. "Okay? See what he's got; what sort of salary; then make up your mind after that."

She returned the brush to the small red box and snapped it closed. "What I didn't get to tell you last night," she said, setting the mascara box on the sink, "is that I'm sort of a crazy person."

"Not at all."

She reached up into the cabinet again and removed a plastic carrying case. "You might not think it, but I am." She unzipped the carrying case and picked up the mascara box and dropped it in.

"What time is it." I looked at my watch. "Get dressed and we'll go over together to Mr. Dupres."

She reached into the cabinet for a tube of toothpaste. "The fainting on the stairway?" she said.

"What about it."

There was a toothbrush in a holder on the wall. "It's not the first time it's happened," she said, lifting it out and putting it in her carrying case.

"So what."

"I mean it's a recurring thing. I should have told you." She walked over to the open shower stall. "I have these things I go through. Sometimes I get depressed for long periods."

I walked over after her. "We all do."

"For maybe a week or ten days," she said, "it'll get worse and worse. Then I'll faint." She looked into the shower stall, then reached in for a cake of soap to drop in the carrying case. "After I regain consciousness I'll feel peaceful again." She stepped back and closed the door of the stall. "For a while."

"Melinda."

She walked back to the medicine cabinet. "But I can see now I should have told you this last night so you would have known I was a loony."

I walked up beside her. "Melinda, you're not a loony."

"I know I'm one. Don't worry about it." She reached up into the medicine cabinet for a tube of lipstick.

"We all have our quirks," I said, "don't you think I do?"

She turned the base of the tube till a pointed end of silverish lipstick came out of the other end. "I'm just saying," she said, leaning up toward the mirror again, "that I'm too unpredictable."

"I don't care."

She moved the lipstick back and forth across her lower lip. "I can't tell what I'm going to do from one minute to the next."

"I don't care."

"Could you hand me another Kleenex?"

I stepped over to the toilet, pulled one up out of the box and handed it to her.

"My first father said I have a mercurial nature." She blotted the tissue against her lower lip.

"That's your strength," I said.

"What he really was trying to say was that I'm a loon." She rubbed the lipstick back and forth over her upper lip. "You'd soon get tired of me," she said, "that's what you don't realize."

I shook my head.

"Everyone does," she said, blotting her upper lip, "they don't realize it at first, then after a while they start getting tired of me and they don't know how to tell me."

I raised my hand up, waited a moment, then rested it on her shoulder. "I'd never get tired of you."

"You don't know."

"I do."

She turned the base of the lipstick tube and the lipstick disappeared back down into the tube. "I know you'd get tired of me," she said, "I even get tired of myself." She dropped the tube into the carrying case.

"Melinda." I reached for her hand. She let me take it and we stood several moments looking into the mirror at the reflection of each other's eyes. "I want to help you," I said.

She shook her head.

"I want to; I do."

"You can't though." She picked up the carrying case and pulled the zipper closed across the top of it.

"I could."

"What do you want to do, marry me?"

"If you want."

She rested her hand on the edge of the sink. "I don't."

"Then I don't want to. I want to help you find a job if

that's what you need," I said. "And in any other way I can."

She turned one of the handles at the other side of the sink and a faucet that had been dripping stopped dripping. "That's thoughtful."

"I mean it." I squeezed her hand.

"But I don't want to stay in Boston," she said. "I've had it in Boston."

"Okay," I said. I was about to say something more when there was a short squeaking sound and the doorknob turned and the door opened and the man with the beard looked in through the crack at us.

"What's happening," he said.

I let go of Melinda's hand and reached over to push the door. "We're talking," I said. The door didn't close. I looked down at the man's shoe in the crack at the bottom. "We'll be finished in a moment."

He looked past me and at Melinda. "What's happening," he said to her.

"Could you just leave us alone for one second?" I said. "We'll be finished in one second."

He looked at me again, then at Melinda. "Get dressed," he said and closed the door.

"I am."

I looked at Melinda. She removed the bathrobe and draped it over the toilet seat. Then she walked to the wall and took a pair of panties and a bra from off a hook. She stepped into the panties and pulled them up, then wrapped the bra around her and snapped it in the back. There was a white slip on the hook beside the first hook. She took it down and put it on. "Melinda," I said.

"I'll write you, Roger."

I let go of the door and went over to her. "Just one thing. Tomorrow. Wait till tomorrow."

"I can't."

She started toward the door and I followed her. "This city," I said. "You say you've had it with Boston?"

"Yes."

Sal opened the door for her and she walked past him and back into the bedroom. I followed her. "Let me take you around," I said. "There's parts of Boston you haven't seen."

"It's just the mood here."

Sal walked back to the chair, seated himself, picked up the magazine and opened it again.

"What mood," I said.

She walked around the bed and to the closet. "People race around too much here." She removed a dress from the closet.

"And you're going to New York?"

"I don't know why," she said, unzipping the dress, "but I feel I have to leave here."

"Stay one more night," I said. "Please."

She lifted the dress up and brought it down over her head. "I'll write to you." Her face was inside the wool dress as she spoke. She brought it down over her shoulders and worked it down across her chest.

"What's wrong with Boston."

"I can't define it." She smoothed the dress down the front of her. "There's just something about it." She straightened up and walked back around the bed. She pulled the door of the bathroom closed so she could look in the mirror.

I followed her, stepping over Sal's legs. "The traffic? Soot? What."

"All those things."

"But they're ten times worse in New York."

She turned to the side and pulled a zipper up along the side of her dress.

"Have you been to Cambridge yet?"

"No."

"It's beautiful. Have you been out to Concord, Lexington, Lincoln; any of these little towns."

She shook her head.

I walked up beside her. "You can't leave without seeing some of these things."

She seated herself on the bed and bent over for a pair of black low-heeled shoes on the carpet. "Roger, I said I'd write you. I meant it."

"Stay."

She bent forward and fitted her foot into one of the shoes. "I'll come back." She picked up the other shoe and fitted her foot into it.

"What about last night," I said. "What about that."

"I won't forget it."

Sal closed his magazine and set it on the table beside his chair. He looked at me, then at Melinda. "Done dressing?"

She nodded.

He got up and walked over to the bed. He picked up the pair of stockings that were draped over the suitcase. "What about these."

"I don't think I'll wear them."

He dropped them into the suitcase, then closed the suitcase and fastened the latches and picked it up from the bed.

"One other thing." Melinda went into the bathroom for her carrying case. Sal opened the suitcase for her to put it in.

"No." I got up from the bed, walked across the room and to the door leading out into the hall. I closed it, then turned the lock. I turned around again and looked at them standing beside each other and looking back at me. "Sal," I said, "last night the two of us got locked into a department store; I don't know if Melinda told you or not." Sal looked at her, then back at me. "Did she tell you that?"

"What's happening," Sal said, gesturing at the door. "What's all this."

"Did she tell you we stayed in the department store."

"She did."

"She told you."

"Roger," Melinda said, "I'll write you tomorrow."

"Did she tell you everything that happened?"

Sal set the suitcase down on the rug beside him. "Wait a minute here," he said.

I took a step toward them. "I've never felt this way before," I said. "I've never acted this way."

Melinda stepped forward and took my hand. "Roger."

"The letter to Beth," I said. "I wrote her this morning. I didn't mention anything about the marriage. I could never go through with it now."

Suddenly Sal pulled her back toward him.

"Let me say one thing to Roger," Melinda said.

"I've never felt this way before," I said.

"Roger."

Sal stepped forward and put his hand between us, then rested the back of his hand on my chest and began pushing me backward. "Hold it," he said, "just hold it."

I braced myself with my foot, reached up and took his wrist. "Sal."

"Just let me say something."

I brought his hand down from my chest. "I'm not a fighter," I said.

"I can see that."

"But I don't like to be pushed."

Melinda picked up the bag and held it out to Sal. "Why don't you wait in the hall."

"One thing," he said. "Just let me say one thing."

"Say it," I said.

Melinda carried the suitcase out into the hall. I followed her.

"I want to say this one thing," Sal said, coming after us.

"What is it."

"Let's get out of here."

Melinda set the bag down on the carpet.

I took her hand again. "The one thing I want to say is that neither of us got much sleep last night. I'm asking you to get a good night's sleep before deciding to leave."

"I did," she said.

Sal took her other hand.

"You didn't."

"I slept all morning when I got back. Roger, I'll write you a long letter tonight. I'll try and explain about myself."

I looked down at the bag, then picked it up. "I want to take this back into the room."

"Will you do something for me? Will you go into the bathroom and get my bathrobe?"

The maid stepped out of one of the doors down the hall and stood looking at us.

"I'll get it," Sal said. "Where is it."

"In the bathroom."

He returned through the door.

"How are you paying for this room," I said. "You said you had four dollars."

"Sal's paying."

I reached into my back pocket for my wallet. "I won't let him."

"He's already paid," she said. "He has a credit card."

"I do too." I pulled out my credit card to show her.

"Roger, I don't want you to take this personally. I'm not leaving because of you."

"But you're not staying because of me."

She took my credit card and my wallet and returned the card into it. "It's not as though we'll never see each other again. Do you ever get down to New York?"

"I never go anywhere."

She handed me back the wallet. "I'll come up here then. Maybe in the summer for a weekend."

I glanced down the hall at the maid. She was still standing just outside the doorway of the other room holding a dustrag. "Melinda," I said quietly, "I don't know what you think of me. You don't think much of me. But after last night. I've never felt this way about anybody; I know how trite that sounds but it's true."

Sal came out of the door with the robe in his hand. "Let's split," he said. He started down the hall ahead of us.

I picked up the suitcase. "All right then," I said. "You take this job."

"We'll be in touch," she said.

"We will." I hurried to catch up with Sal. "Sal?"

"What's happening."

"I'm going to have them transfer her bill onto my credit card."

"What's that." He kept walking.

"Melinda's bill. I'm going to have them transfer it from your credit card onto my credit card."

"What for."

"Because I want to."

He shrugged and kept walking.

I stopped long enough to let Melinda catch up with me. "I just told Sal. I'm going to have them put your bill on my card."

"Thank you."

I walked along beside her. "You don't have my address," I said.

"What is it."

I set down the suitcase and opened my wallet again. "Do you have a pencil?"

"I don't."

"I just have a piece of paper." Sal turned a corner ahead of us. "Maybe he does." I picked up the bag and started after him, walking around the corner just as the door of one of the three elevators there opened. Sal put his foot in it to hold it. "Thank you." I walked in and set the suitcase down beside an older woman. Melinda came around the corner and followed me in, then Sal came in and the door closed. "Sal," I said, "do you have a pen or pencil."

He shook his head.

"Ma'am," I said, "by any chance do you have a pen or pencil."

"Me?"

"Yes."

She looked at me a moment, then opened her purse.

I turned toward Melinda. "I'll give you the travel agency number and the apartment number. I'm usually at the travel agency till five-thirty, then at the apartment after six."

"Give me both of them," she said.

"I will." I turned back to the lady. She was holding a plastic pencil in her hand and twisting the top of it. "Thank you," I said.

"I think it's out of lead."

The elevator stopped, the door came open and a man came in with a woman.

"The lead must have fallen out into my purse," she said.

"Could you look for it."

She opened her purse again and began rummaging around in it. "I'll never find it in here."

The elevator doors closed.

"Can I look."

"I'd rather you didn't."

"A pen," I said to the man who had just come in. "Do you have a pen I could borrow." He reached into the inside of his coat, there was a click and his hand came out with a fountain pen.

"Thank you." I took it and unscrewed the cap. "Let's see what this is." I opened up the piece of paper I had removed from my wallet and looked on the other side. "This is my receipt for the telephone," I said. "If you could send it back it would help me get the deposit back."

"I'll do that," Melinda said.

I turned around and opened the piece of paper up against the wall of the elevator. The elevator stopped. I glanced around as four ladies stepped on. Then the doors closed and we started down again. "Here's the agency address and phone." I wrote it down at the top of the page. "I'm there Saturdays till noon also; as well as the weekdays. Let me jot that down." I wrote down Sat.'s till noon under the address and phone number. "Now my apartment."

The elevator stopped again. "I have to get off here," someone said.

"I'm here evenings. After six I'm almost always here."

"Sir?" The man who had loaned me the pen was holding out his hand. "We have to get off here."

"Just one second." I began writing down the address and phone of the apartment. The man kept his arm in the door of the elevator so that the door started closed, hit his arm, jerked, opened, started closed again, jerked and opened again and started closed again. "Saturday afternoons I might be here or I might not. Sundays; can't tell." I removed the piece of paper from the wall and looked at it. "I'll just jot my name," I said, returning it to the wall. "Sometimes people spell the last one wrong." I wrote my name at the top of the page.

"Thank you," the man said, holding his hand out.

I screwed the top of the pen back on and handed it to him.

I handed the receipt to Melinda. "If you could copy down the information and send this back."

"I will."

"Good."

We rode silently the rest of the way down, till the car stopped at the bottom and the doors opened into the lobby. Sal went out first, carrying the bathrobe, then I followed with the suitcase.

"Don't worry about things," Melinda said.

"I won't."

We walked around an old man sitting in a chair. "About last night," she said. "Don't get the impression it didn't mean anything to me. It did."

"It did?"

She went on one side of a pillar and I went on the other. "I wouldn't have done that with just anybody," she said when we came back together. "It might seem to you like I'm the kind of person who would have."

"You wouldn't have though."

Sal went ahead out of the front doors of the hotel. "I don't want you to think I would have."

I hurried ahead of Melinda and held open the door, holding her suitcase aside so she could pass. "What are you saying," I said.

"I'm saying please don't hate me."

I followed her and let the door close behind us. "You wouldn't have done it with just anybody."

"No."

I hurried around to be on the street side of her. "Just with me."

"I don't want you to think I used you."

"Listen," I said, transferring the suitcase to my other hand as I walked, "it seems like we should talk."

"Sal's car's not for a block."

"But I mean in depth," I said. "You're racing off. How do you know you won't regret it."

"I don't."

We walked around a woman leading a dog on a leash.

"I don't want you to go," I said. "I don't think you really want to go either."

"I may not."

"You don't." We turned around a corner. "Listen. Tell Sal I'll pay for his accommodations here for one night. We'll go and talk. Tomorrow you'll have perspective."

Ahead of us Sal was opening the door of a small dirty white convertible next to the curb. Its top was down. He tossed the bathrobe into the back seat, got in and inserted his keys into the ignition switch. He turned the motor on, then felt around on the other side of the steering wheel. A moment later there was a whirring sound, then the top began rising up from behind the back seat to cover the car, dropping some leaves beside the car as it moved. We reached the car and Melinda opened the front door. "Just stick the bag in front."

"Sal," I said, "I'd like to suggest an alternate plan."

Melinda took the bag. "Goodbye," she said. She put her hand on my face and kissed me. "I'm not going to forget you," she said. "Don't worry."

"I just want to tell Sal the alternate plan," I said. "Sal?"

"What's happening." He was looking back over his shoulder as the black canvas top, crackling slightly, reached the top of its ascent and began moving slowly down. Melinda got into the car.

"We really haven't talked," I said, "yet we have a great number of things to talk about."

Suddenly the whirring noise stopped and the car's top stopped where it was. "Shit," Sal said. He reached up and tugged on it.

"Spend the night here in Boston," I said.

He bent sideways and began pushing at the button on the other side of the steering wheel.

"Sal?"

"I can't, man, I've got to get back to the city."

"What's wrong with the roof," Melinda said.

"It sticks."

Melinda reached up to tug on it.

"Don't pull it," Sal said. "It'll bust."

Melinda let go of it.

"Have you eaten lunch yet?" I said.

Melinda turned in the seat and held out her hand and I took it. "I have your addresses," she said.

"Let me buy the two of you a good lunch."

Sal straightened up in his seat. "Sometimes the bastard goes down if I get moving." He began revving up the engine; clouds of gray smoke rose up from behind the car.

"Goodbye," Melinda said.

"This doesn't seem right."

I kept a hold of her hand as Sal backed the car several feet, his bumper hitting the car in back, then I hurried forward, still holding her hand, as he drove up and his front bumper hit the car ahead. "Sal," I said, "what's your address. Your business."

"Let me get out of here first." He backed up again and I stepped down off the curb and walked along beside the car, holding Melinda's hand, then stopped when the car stopped and walked forward again. I let go of Melinda's hand and jumped back just before the rear of the car came around and moved out of the parking place.

"Your business address?" I said.

The car continued slowly on down the street, the canvas top up at an angle over their heads. At the corner it turned and I watched as they disappeared out of sight.

I stood a few moments looking after them, then turned and walked back up onto the sidewalk. I stopped next to the parking meter beside the empty space. It was still ticking. Just as I was standing beside it there was a loud click; I looked down just as a small red sign came up in the other side of the glass reading VIOLATION. Then I put my hands in my pocket and began walking slowly back toward the travel agency.

3

I'M RESPONSIBLE for keeping the office clean. The first day I came to work Mr. Becker asked me if I'd object to keeping the place up and I said I wouldn't. He showed me how, and from then on I did it.

Usually I try to get in by eight-thirty. There is an ashtray on my desk, even though I don't smoke, which I empty, and there is a floor ashtray over by the waiting couch, which I also empty. After these are emptied I go into the back room, which is a bathroom, and bring out the push broom and carpet sweeper, which are kept beside the toilet. First I use the broom to sweep the floor. I open the door and sweep the pile out and across the sidewalk and into the gutter. If there is any debris on the sidewalk in front I pick it up and put it in the wastebasket. Then I come back in and run the carpet sweeper over the two rugs. When this is done I take the push broom and the sweeper back into the bathroom and lean them up against the wall again.

There are other things I do, such as dusting off the desk tops and the tables, but I don't do this every day. I also wash the front windows and the glass in the door but this is necessary only once every week. The wastebasket needs to be emptied into a trash barrel around behind the building in an alley and I do this each evening before I go, since the trash collectors come early in the morning. I have never minded doing these jobs and had never given it much thought.

Then I stopped doing it. I can't say I know why. The first morning I stopped was the morning after I had stayed in the department store all night with Melinda. It was almost nine when I got out of the store; I stopped off to have a doughnut and a cup of coffee before going to the travel agency, and then when I got there the first thing I did was to write the letter to Beth. It occurred to me that I should have been cleaning up, but I didn't. I was sure I would do it the next morning and that it wouldn't make too much difference. I remember looking up halfway through my letter to Beth and noticing a large black ground-out cigar in the ashtray beside the door and thinking of emptying it. Next morning, though, the morning after Melinda left, the ground-out cigar was still in the ashtray. I sat at my desk from about eight-thirty until nine looking at it. At nine I got up and went to the door and opened it, then went back to my desk. A few minutes later a man and a woman stopped in front, then came in through the door.

"Is Mr. Becker here?" the man said.

"He'll be back next week."

The man glanced down at a crumpled piece of paper that had fallen off the edge of the desk onto the floor, then back at me. "We'll come back next week, thank you." They turned around and left.

I sat at the desk all morning without getting up, except once to go to the bathroom. There was one phone call from a woman wanting to know how much it cost to fly to Hawaii. At about ten-thirty I opened the drawer and got out a folder for Mr. and Mrs. Keystone, then removed some sheets of paper and carbon paper from the other drawer, assembled them and put them in the typewriter. I typed out Keystone Itinerary at the top of the page, but then stopped and didn't type anything more. I looked at what I had typed for a while, then swiveled around in the chair and sat looking out at the sidewalk.

At about one o'clock I went down to the coffee shop and bought a hot dog and brought it back and ate it at the desk. Then I waited some more.

Sometime around three o'clock in the afternoon I went to stand in the doorway and look out at the traffic, and at the people passing. Sometime later I returned to the desk, sat down and pulled the phone in front of me. I dialed the number for information in New York. "Do you have a listing for Sal Hobbes," I said, when a girl answered. "It might be a Sal Hobbes Advertising Agency, or it might just be a residence."

"One moment please."

I waited a few moments, till she came back. "Hobbes?" she said. "H-O-B-B-E-S?"

"Yes."

"We show no such listing," she said.

"Sal."

"There's no Sal."

I picked up a pencil on the desk in front of me. "How many Hobbes are there."

"Over a hundred."

"But no Sal?"

"No, sir."

I waited awhile longer, listening into the phone, looking down at the point of my pencil as it rested on a sheet of scrap paper on the desk. "Sir?" she said finally.

"Thank you; goodbye."

I spent the rest of the afternoon sitting in the chair, looking at a poster on the wall.

At the end of the day when I left the office the sheets of paper were still in the typewriter with Keystone Itinerary typed at the top of the page. The typewriter cover had slipped down onto the floor during the afternoon. I looked down at it, then walked across the room and out the door. I closed the door, checked to be sure it was locked and started along the sidewalk.

I have always thought fall was the best season. Next to fall I like spring. Usually during these two seasons, when I finished work, I would walk up to the Common, about four blocks from the travel agency. To get to my apartment it was shorter to skirt by the Common but in fall and spring I usually took about ten extra minutes to walk through it. On that day, because it was spring, and because I was in the habit, I walked up toward the Common after work, waited at the stoplight, then crossed and stepped up on the opposite curb and started down the main path. There are trees on both sides of the paths and in the center the main path intersects with a wide path that crosses the Common from the other side. There is a pond and some benches there where I sometimes used to sit. After I had passed only three or four trees, however, I stopped and didn't go farther. I waited a moment, then turned around and started back, walking quickly. I came to the street again and turned. I walked along in the street for a while, then when there was a break in the traffic I hurried across to the other side and stepped up onto the opposite sidewalk. At the end of the block there was a red light but there weren't any cars coming so I ran across.

My apartment was on the third story of a brick apartment building partway up Beacon Hill. As I approached it, I took my key from my pocket, crossed the street to the right side, squeezed between my Volkswagen and another car and walked up the front steps. I walked in through the first door and inserted my key in the lock.

No one was downstairs, just the table beside the foot of the stairs with a plastic fern in a pot. I ran up the first flight of stairs, turned and ran up the second and to my door. I found the right key and put it in the lock and turned it. There was a click and the door opened. I pulled the key out and went inside.

What I usually did when I got home was to go to the other side of the room, where there was a large slightly curved window, and push it open, since it got musty during the day. But instead of this I went to the closet and opened it and removed a small suitcase. I carried it past the kitchenette and into the bedroom and set it on my bed, then went to the bedroom closet. I bent over to get an extra pair of shoes from the floor. I took them to the bed and set them in the bottom of the suitcase. Then I went to the bureau and opened the top drawer. I took out a pair of socks and a folded white shirt, closed the drawer and opened the next one down. There was a pile of undershorts on one side; I removed the top pair. On the other side were several ties, each of them rolled and placed next to the other. I looked at them a moment, then selected one near the center of the group. I pushed the drawer closed and carried the things to the bed and set them in the suitcase. After closing the suitcase I looked around the room a moment, then walked back out through the living room and through the door, back down the two flights of stairs and outside to my Volkswagen, getting the keys out of my pocket and arranging the Volkswagen key to be ready to insert it into the car's door handle as I walked.

It wasn't far from my apartment to the turnpike, and it took about eight or nine minutes to drive there, going down to Commonwealth Avenue and getting on the interchange at Copley Square. At the entrance to the turnpike there are booths. I handed my nickel and dime through my window to the attendant, then drove onto the turnpike.

I would say it is approximately eight or nine miles from downtown to the outskirts of the city, and takes about ten minutes to get there. Then there are more booths. I turned slightly to be headed into the one on the left. There was a truck ahead that went through, its driver reaching out the window for a ticket before he drove on. Then the car ahead of me drove up beside the booth and its driver reached out for his ticket. His hand went back into his car and he moved on. I waited a moment, then drove up beside the booth. A man, smiling, stopped halfway out of the booth and held out a ticket. "Good evening," he said. I looked out my window at the ticket in his hand. "Good evening," he said. He moved the ticket an inch closer to my window.

I looked up into his face. "This is pointless," I said.

After a moment he stepped farther out of his booth and bent partway over, still holding the ticket out toward me. "I don't hear you."

"I was going to New York to find this person," I said, "but I don't know where to look. I don't know where to begin."

He lowered the ticket slightly but continued looking in at me. The car behind me raced its motor.

"I thought I could go down there and find her, but there's no reason to think I could." I looked down at my steering wheel.

"Sir, please take your ticket now."

I looked up into my mirror. "What am I thinking."

He held up the ticket again. "Here, sir."

I reached up and took it, then I stepped on the accelerator.

I drove slowly to the Framingham off-ramp, turned and went around in a curve till I came to more booths. I stopped beside one and handed my ticket and twenty cents to a man. Then I drove on and down a hill, under an underpass, and up around a curve to a new booth. A man stepped out and gave me a ticket. I drove onto the turnpike again and back to the entrance of the turnpike with the first set of booths. I drove up beside one of them and a man stepped out, smiling. "Good evening," he said.

I handed him my ticket and twenty cents, then drove on through and into the fast lane going back to Boston.

I don't remember exactly which day the long-distance phone call came. I think it was the fifth day after Melinda had left. I was sitting in the chair at the desk, looking at the phone, when it rang.

I picked up the receiver before it had finished the first ring. "Yes?"

There was a static sound coming out of it. Then the voice of an operator. "Hello?" she said.

"Go ahead."

"Long distance calling a Mr. Roger Hart."

I moved my chair up to the desk. "Go ahead." I pressed the receiver tighter against my ear. No one spoke for several moments; there was just the sound of the static. I rested my other hand on the desk and began tapping on the desk surface with one of my fingers. I cleared my throat. Still there was no voice. "Hello," I said finally. "Operator?"

"Just a moment, sir. We're having some trouble with the transmission of the call."

I moved the phone around to my other ear.

"Can you hold?" she said.

"Yes."

I waited awhile longer, then suddenly the static was interrupted by a loud crackling sound. I moved the receiver slightly away from my ear, then returned it when the sound had stopped. "Sir?"

"Yes."

"We're having some transmission difficulties on your call from Ceylon," she said, "can you hold?"

I looked down at my hand resting on the desk. "Excuse me?"

"Can you hold."

"My call from where?"

"Ceylon," she said.

There was some more crackling, not as loud as before. I moved the receiver back around to the other ear again.

"Sir? Hello?"

"Yes."

"We're ready," she said. "I think we're ready. Can we go ahead now on your call from Ceylon?"

"Go ahead."

There was a crackling sound of a slightly different kind than before, then a new voice, a woman's, coming very faintly through the noise. "Hello?" it said.

I pressed the receiver harder against my ear. "Hello!"

She said something else.

"I can't hear you!" I pressed my other hand over the other ear.

She said something else, but I still couldn't understand it.

I got up, went to the door and pushed it closed, then went back to the chair and picked up the receiver again.

"I just shut the door; go ahead."

"Mr. Hart?"

"Yes."

The voice was still very faint but by pressing my other hand over my other ear and keeping my eyes shut I could barely make it out. "This is Amelia Becker calling," she said, "from Ceylon."

"Oh."

"Mrs. Becker."

"Yes."

There was some crackling. "Paul has had . . ." More crackling.

"Mrs. Becker . . . I can't . . ."

Even though the voice was still faint I could tell she was nearly shouting into her telephone. "Mr. Becker has had a heart attack."

"Oh no."

A new burst of crackling.

"Oh God."

"Mr. Hart?"

"Yes."

"A heart attack two days ago in the dining room of the hotel."

"Is he . . . "

She said something I couldn't hear.

I transferred the phone around to the other ear. "Repeat please?"

"He's in the hospital. At first they didn't know if he was going to . . ." A sudden burst of new crackling. ". . . but now they're pretty sure he will."

"Thank God."

"But he can't be moved. We have to stay right here."

"I'm so sorry, Mrs. Becker."

After another silence, there was the voice of the operator again. "Is that Ceylon call coming along all right?"

"Yes," I said, "my boss had a heart attack."

"I'm sorry."

I cleared my throat. "Mrs. Becker?"

There was a long silence, then finally she spoke. "Mr. Hart, we're in the hospital now. They're going to hold the phone up to him. He can just say one or two words; he wanted to so badly. Just for a second though."

I moved the earpiece of the receiver so that it was centered more squarely over my ear. I heard his wife's voice through the static. "Just say hello to him," she said, "don't try and say any more than that."

Extremely faintly, Mr. Becker's voice came through the static. "Roger?"

"Sir," I said. "I don't . . . I don't know what to say."

"A damn thing to happen."

His wife's voice: "That's enough; all right."

"Just let me ask him . . ."

"I'll ask him." His wife cleared her throat. "Roger?"

"Yes Mrs. Becker."

"Everything's going well at the agency?"

"Oh yes."

"Some new customers?"

"New ones," I said, "old ones, return business. Things are humming along."

"You can carry on a little longer by yourself?"

I nodded. "Tell him I can carry on."

"Goodbye, Roger."

"I'm so sorry about this."

A new crackling sound. "Just so he knows everything's under control back there."

"Tell him not to worry."

There was a change in the tone of the crackling, then the voice of the operator. "Hello?" she said.

"Yes."

"Did you complete your call from Ceylon."

"Yes, thank you." I moved the receiver down from my ear and toward the cradle of the telephone but then heard the operator say something more. I returned it back up to my ear. "Excuse me?"

"I'm sorry I butted in; I thought you might have been having difficulties."

"My boss had a heart attack."

"It's awful."

"Goodbye. Thank you." I hung up the phone.

I sat for about five minutes with my hand on the receiver of the phone, then looked up. The first thing I saw was the ashtray by the door with the black ground-out cigar butt still in it and several ground-out cigarette butts that had been left during the morning by Mr. Birkhausen while he was waiting for his itinerary. I pushed the chair back from the desk and got up and walked over to the ashtray. It was on a bronze stand with a large glass dish on the top for the ashes and butts. By turning the dish slightly, it came loose from the stand. I lifted it up and carried it across the room into the back room. I emptied it into a large paper box on top of some crumpled newspapers, then turned on the water in the sink and held the dish under it. There was a sponge on the edge of the sink. I got it wet, then rubbed it around on the dish till all the ashes were gone and the glass was clean. I took a paper towel down from a towel dispenser on the wall, crushed it into a ball and dried out the dish. Then I dropped the towel into the carton.

Against the wall was a push broom. On a hook on the wall was a dustrag. I picked up the broom and removed the rag and returned into the other room. After putting the dish back on its stand I walked over to the corner of the room and began sweeping. I swept for about two minutes, till I'd accumulated a pile of dirt and a crumpled piece of carbon paper. Then I looked down at the carbon paper for a moment, leaned the broom handle against the wall and walked back to the desk. There was a film of dust covering the desk and the typewriter. I looked down at the rag in my hand. I stood for quite a long time looking down at the rag and at the dust on the typewriter. Then, very slowly, I eased myself back down into the chair again. I rested my hand and the rag in my lap and sat there for the rest of the afternoon.

That evening I went out to the dog racing track in Revere.

I had never been to a dog race before. The reason I found out about it was that during the afternoon a man came into the agency with a stack of signs and said he would pay me ten dollars if he could display one of them in our window for a month. I said he could and took ten dollars. He set the sign up in the window against the glass and left. When he was gone I got up and went to the window and picked up the cardboard sign and turned it around to see a picture of a greyhound dog and a bundle of money. It said, "They're running at Revere, 8:00 nightly." I turned the sign around and put it back against the window.

It took me about forty minutes to drive out there, leaving after dinner. Most of the drive was on the expressway, which was very crowded. As I got close to Revere the traffic became bumper-to-bumper and just before coming to the turnoff I had to sit in one place for about ten minutes without moving. There were policemen standing at the turnoff motioning the cars to turn off. I turned and drove down the ramp. At the bottom there was a large cardboard sign nailed to a tree that said DOG TRACK on it and had an arrow. I drove under an underpass and continued slowly along. A newspaper boy came up beside the car and stuck a newspaper in through the window. "No," I said, but he kept it in front of my nose till I began moving forward again.

I went past rows of old apartment buildings, most of them wooden or with tarpaper coverings, the tarpaper made to look like red bricks or gray or yellow. Children sat out in the dirt in front of most of the buildings, watching the cars. Then there was an old bus station and the road turned, and I drove along the beach for a while and then came to the track.

The parking lot was across the street from the track with an old man standing in the entranceway waving for the cars to come in. I put on my blinker and turned. The old man slapped his hand against the side of my car and pointed down toward the end of the lot. I drove past several rows of parked cars, turned into one of the aisles, then into a space. I got out and started back toward the street. Then I stopped, went back to the car and locked it, then started toward the street again.

It was just before eight o'clock and the people were pouring out of the parking lot. I walked to the street and waited while a crowd formed, then a policeman waded into the traffic, holding out his arms and shouting at the drivers of the cars, and they stopped and the people who had collected at the side of the street found their way between the bumpers of the cars and to the other side. There was an entranceway and then some turnstiles, lines forming behind them. The people moved slowly up toward an old man waiting to take their money. I had my money ready when I got to him and gave it to him and went through the turnstile inside.

An old man was standing beside a table selling programs. I stopped and bought one from him. "Where do you go," I said.

"For what."

"To see the race."

He spat, then pointed off past a large refreshment stand, with people crowding around it.

"Thanks."

I walked past the refreshment stand, opening my program to look inside. There was an ad for Coca-Cola inside the cover, but it hadn't been printed right on the center of the page so that the girl's face was halfway up off the top with only her nose and mouth left on the page. A fat man bumped against me from the side. I closed the program, reached behind me to touch the pocket with the wallet in it and kept walking toward the track. It was crowded and noisy and there was loud music coming from out of loudspeakers mounted on concrete posts that supported the roof. I walked past rows of benches where people sat looking over programs. Beyond them was an outdoor area where more people milled around, then a wire fence and the track on the other side of it.

On the grass in the center of the track were several large painted plywood models of greyhound dogs propped up in a row. I looked out at them for a few moments, then back at the rows of benches where the people sat with their programs. Past them were tellers' windows, people lined up behind them. I watched a man hand some money through a window and get a ticket. He walked away with it and the next man handed money through and got a ticket back. There was a brief moment of silence as one song ended, then another loud one began, played on an organ. I looked back down at my program and opened it again. I turned past the first page, then the second, then on the next page it said First Race at the top. Underneath was a list of names with information after each name. I ran my eyes down across the names. The fifth name down was Big Ned. I stopped and read across. The dog weighed fifty-two pounds. After its weight it said, "Wet track could cause trouble, otherwise this one may go." I looked back out at the track. It didn't look wet. Someone bumped me from behind. I stepped aside, felt my wallet, then looked over at the betting windows again. The lines were getting longer. I found my way between two of the benches and to the end of a line, then waited. It took several minutes to work my way up. When it was my turn I held the program up so the man behind could see it and said, "Big Ned please."

The man tipped his head up slightly as though he hadn't heard.

"A bet on Big Ned please."

"Two dollars to win?"

"Please." I removed my wallet and took out two dollars to hand to him.

"Just give the dog's numbers after this," he said, handing me a ticket. "Don't show me your program."

"Sorry."

"We got to keep them moving."

I stepped aside and put the ticket in the pocket of my coat. I was just about to start walking back down toward the track when I noticed a man standing off by one of the concrete supports watching me. He was wearing a gray jacket with its zipper open, his hands in its pockets. As I looked over and noticed that he was looking at me, he smiled and removed one of his hands from his pockets. The refreshment stand was off in the other direction. I started off toward it. I glanced sideways once and noticed that he had left his place by the concrete support and was walking between two of the benches and toward me. I turned slightly so that I would make a wider circle to get to the stand, but then glanced over to see him moving faster. He changed his direction slightly so we were headed toward the same point. I decided to keep going and walk past him and up to the stand, but as we approached he held out his hand again. "Hey, Charlie," he said.

I walked past him.

"Hey, fella."

I felt him put his hand on my back. I turned around. "Yes?"

He was smiling. "Having a good time?"

"Yes."

"Good," he said. "Say, I just wanted to tell you about Harry's Hero in the next race."

"Oh?"

"Number four," he said. He reached out and took my program. "Let's see." He turned to the next page. "Here it is." He pointed to Harry's Hero.

"Oh yes."

"Don't pass it up." He handed me back the program.

"Thanks."

He put his hands back in his pockets but stepped up closer beside me. "Getting a hot dog?" he said.

I glanced over at the stand, then back at him. "I thought I'd have a beer."

"My treat?"

"No, I'll buy it."

He grinned.

I looked back at him a few moments, then started turning away. "Thanks for the tip, I appreciate it."

"Hey," he said. He stepped up even closer so that his face was only several inches away from mine, then he cleared his throat. "I've got a nice little thing over there on the bench," he said quietly.

Someone bumped me from the other direction so that I moved even closer to him. "I didn't hear you," I said.

He motioned with his head. "Over there."

I looked where he was motioning.

"See it?"

"See what."

"The fifth bench," he said. "Right in the middle. Reading the newspaper."

I looked along the benches. At the fifth bench I looked in past the people working over their programs till I saw a woman with red hair and a green sweater sitting, looking down at a newspaper on her lap. "Oh," I said.

"Thirty dollars," the man said quietly.

"Oh, no."

"Twenty-five."

I stepped away from him. "It's not the money," I said. "It's just that I came to watch the races." I turned toward the refreshment stand.

He stepped around in front of me. "She liked your looks," he said. "She told me, 'Go see who that kid is for me. Tell him I'll do nice things for him.' "

"Well you thank her." I stepped around him and up to an opening in front of the counter. "A beer please?"

The man was still right beside me. "She'll do things you won't believe," he said. "Twenty bucks for you because you look clean."

"I guess not, thank you." I turned away so my back was to him.

"She saw you come in the gate and she told me she didn't want no one else."

The girl behind the counter removed a large paper cup from a stack of cups and held it under a spout. She pressed down a handle and waited till beer had filled it and a cap of foam rose up from the top of the cup. Then she took a small piece of wood and scraped off the foam and held out the cup to me. "Fifty cents."

I handed her fifty cents.

"Thank you."

I turned and started down toward the track. The man stayed beside me. "What do you say," he said.

"I say I'm not interested." I took a sip of the beer as I walked.

"I didn't tell you my name," the man said. "It's Rick. Her name's Joanna."

I stopped and turned toward him. "I came to see the races; that's all. Maybe someone else here would like to do it with her but I've never been to a dog race before." I turned

and started down toward the track again. As I was halfway
down, the music stopped and a voice came out of the speaker:
"Two minutes to post time," it said.

The area in front of the track was becoming more
crowded and there was no space left right up along the fence.
Holding the beer up close to my chest, I moved slowly between the other figures and closer to the track. A sloping
area of concrete led down to the fence. I got nearly down to
the bottom of it, then stopped. There was a layer of blue
smoke hanging over the people's heads. I looked behind me
but the man who had spoken to me was gone.

In the center of the track, by the plywood dogs, was a
board with some numbers on it, then, at the end of the track,
a row of metal stalls. Just as I was looking at them, several
men came up from behind leading the dogs by their collars.
They removed the short leashes, pushed them into the stalls
and closed the doors. I was close enough so that I could hear
some scratching inside the stalls, then some whimpering;
then the men who had brought the dogs up turned around
and walked away. I took another sip of the beer and moved
a few steps closer to the fence, fitting myself between two
people so I could rest my hand on top of the railing. The
man beside me had several tickets spread into a fan, which
he was studying. I brought my ticket out and looked at it.
The music stopped again, then came a voice. "Ladies and
gentlemen, welcome to the races. It's a good night for dog
races and we have some good hounds for you and we don't
want to waste any time." Suddenly the voice stopped, and a
very high and shrill woman's voice came out of the loudspeakers singing "The Star-Spangled Banner" quickly. The
man next to me took his hat off while she was singing it,
scratched his head right after she had finished and put the

hat back on. "All right then," the voice said. I felt people
pressing in behind me toward the fence. "And here he
comes, folks," the voice said. "There goes Swifty." I looked
down the track and saw coming around the corner a small
white object on the end of a metal pole. It moved past the
stalls and, just as it did, the stall doors flipped open and
the greyhounds leaped out of the boxes and started chasing
the white object. "They're out!" The white object picked up
speed as it came toward us. It made a whirring sound as the
pole which it was fastened onto moved quickly along in its
runway. "Big Ned in an early lead."

"That's my dog," I said aloud. I looked down at the number 5 on my ticket, then up at the dogs as they ran past.
They each had a piece of cloth draped over their backs with
a number on it. The one in front was a light brown color
and its number was 5. "My dog," I said. I pressed up closer
to the fence. There was a thumping sound as they sped past
and ran on.

"Still Big Ned," the man said.

I tightened my hand around the ticket. "Go!"

"Royal Sir is second," the voice said, "and then Delilah,
but Big Ned is way out there and widening that lead around
the first turn."

I took a swallow of the beer. "Go, Big Ned, go," I said
quietly. On the other side of the track another dog came up
even with Big Ned, then moved a little ahead. It got even
farther ahead as they ran along the straight part of the track
on the other side. While they were running over there, a
man pushed his way up beside me to the fence holding a pair
of binoculars up to his eyes. "Tiny Joe, you bitch," he said,
"run!"

"Go, Ned," I said.

The crowd started yelling more as the dogs came around

the turn where they had first started. They were breathing heavily as they ran past us, their tongues hanging out of their mouths. Ned and the other dog were just even. The false rabbit sped along in front, whirring as it passed us, then the dogs leaped across the finish line. A large length of canvas suddenly stretched across the track on a pole so that all the dogs tumbled into it and fell down. The false rabbit continued on around the track. I watched the dogs roll around then pick themselves up, and then I looked down at my ticket, which was bent slightly. "I think I won," I said.

"Big Ned is the winner," the voice said, "with Happiness running second and Royal Sir to show."

"I won," I said. The crush of people against the fence had loosened up. The man with the binoculars was walking back up toward the grandstands. He shook his head and spat as he walked. "Excuse me," I said, walking up behind him. "Where do you get your money." He didn't hear me but continued walking, spitting again.

I moved up with the others across the open space, and it was just as I was passing by one of the supports of the roof that the man in the gabardine jacket appeared beside a green trash barrel several yards away. "How'd you make out," he said.

"I won."

He stepped forward, raising his eyebrows. "Yeah?"

I held up the ticket. "I had Big Ned."

"Jesus," he said, "let's see."

I held the ticket up so he could see the 5.

"Don't flash that around, son." He put his hand over the ticket and pushed it back down. "If you've got a winning ticket, don't flash it."

I held it in close to myself. "I was just looking for the place to get the money."

"Come with me." He turned and touched my elbow to in-
dicate for me to go ahead of him. "I'm not saying anyone
would snatch it," he said, guiding me up past the refreshment stand, "but you never know. These crowds, you never
know who's in them." We stepped around a small crowd of
men talking. "What's your name."

"Roger."

"Roger," he said, "I felt kind of bad about what happened
before."

Someone pushed in front of us carrying a hot dog in each
hand.

"I think you might have got the wrong impression about
Joanna."

"It's all right."

"What I'm saying, though, I'm saying that she's not a pro,
nothing like that."

We stepped around a bench.

"Very selective," he said. "She just happened to see you
coming in; I'm a good friend of hers; she said she liked your
looks, that you looked like you came from a good family, and
that's why I came up." He guided me to the side and around
the end of a row of booths where the men were selling tickets. "I don't want you to feel I'm putting on any pressure."

"Oh no."

"If you wanted to go over and just talk to her a minute, I
know she'd like to meet you." Around on the other side of the
tellers' windows was another row of windows with lines beginning to form behind them. "Line up here." He guided me
to the end of the nearest line. "I guess you wouldn't want to
just go over and say hello; she'd like to meet you but I don't
want you to feel like there's any pressure."

I stepped forward as the man in front of me moved ahead.
"It's just that I came here primarily to see the races."

The man held up his hand. "Don't get me wrong. I want you to enjoy yourself."

I nodded.

"No pressure."

"Some other time, you know, it might have been different."

"I get you."

"Some other place."

He held his hand up slightly higher. "Say no more, friend. I'll go up with you, see that you get your money okay, and that's it. We'll part friends." I stepped another two spaces up in line. "Keep that ticket held real tight."

I moved it in closer to my chest.

"That's it, now you're talking."

In about another half minute the line had moved up to the window. Rick was standing beside me. "This gentleman has a two-dollar ticket on Big Ned," he said through the bars. "Pay him off, will you?"

"Ticket please," the man said.

I slid it under the bars.

Rick was pointing up at some figures on a card taped beside the window. "Here's how much you get," he said. "Eighteen dollars and thirty cents."

The man pushed a small stack of bills under the bars and then three dimes.

"Count it now," Rick said. "Don't take any chances."

I counted it quickly. "It's all there."

"Well look." He patted my arm. "Anything else you need, don't hesitate."

"Thank you."

"Have a good time."

I removed a dollar from the top of my stack. "Can I give you this for your trouble?"

He held his hand up again. "I don't want your money," he said. "I came up so's you'd know there weren't any bad feelings between us. Have a good time, pick more winners, take her easy, right?"

"Appreciate it."

He turned around and walked away past the people who had been waiting in the line behind us. Then he turned around the corner, reaching into the pocket of his jacket for a package of cigarettes as he walked.

It was just after he was out of sight I noticed across the open space and against the wall that there was a row of phone booths. It was the first time I had noticed them. "Beth," I said when I saw them. Two men, walking and talking, jostled me from behind. I continued looking over at the booths for a few moments after they had passed, then turned and walked to the refreshment stand again.

My beer cup was empty. After waiting till there was a space between the other customers I held it out toward the girl who had waited on me before. "Another beer please."

She looked at the cup. "What's this."

"My cup."

She looked at my face a moment, then turned toward a man behind her who was flipping over a row of hot dogs on a griddle. "Lou?"

He flipped over several more, then looked at her. "Huh?"

"He brought his cup back," she said, pointing at me.

"Who?"

"He brought his cup back," she said. "Should I use it again or give him a new one."

Lou stepped over with his spatula and removed the cup from my hand. "Don't bring your cup back," he said to me. He dropped it in a trash barrel. "You never use the old cup. Give him a new one." He went back to the griddle.

The girl removed a new cup from the stack and held it under the spout till it filled with beer.

"I have a phone call to make," I said as she scraped off the foam. "I wonder if I could get some change." I handed her four of the dollar bills I had gotten from the man behind the bars. "It's a call to Wisconsin."

"Quarters?"

"Please."

She went to the change box, counted out the change and handed it to me. "Thank you." I took a sip of the beer so it wouldn't be so full, then started working my way through the crowd toward the booths.

There were six booths and all but two of them were being used. I started into one of the empty ones, then noticed that the phone was practically wrenched off the wall, the receiver was hanging down on its cord. Someone had scotch-taped a small "out of order" sign on the dial. I stepped back out and went into the one beside it, then sat down and rested my beer on the shelf. I didn't have any dimes so I put a quarter in and dialed the operator, taking a sip of the beer while I was waiting. "Person-to-person to Beth Knudsen," I said when she answered. "That's in the dormitory of the Thomasville Nursing School in Thomasville, Wisconsin."

"Do you have the phone number?"

"I don't, no."

I took another sip of the beer and waited, looking out through the glass of the phone-booth door. The music was playing again. I looked up at a green loudspeaker mounted atop one of the concrete supports, then across the rows of benches. Nearly all were filled with people bent over programs. I took another swallow of beer and returned the cup to the shelf. On the end of the first bench a man sat holding a white sack in his lap, eating a sandwich. I counted back to

the fifth bench. My eyes slid along the bench to the center.
A man was leaning back with his hat over his eyes. Beside
him sat an old lady in a black coat, and next to her was an
empty space. By raising up slightly from my seat I could see
that a newspaper had been left there in the place where the
girl Joanna had been before. "Two dollars and thirty cents
for the first three minutes."

I began dropping quarters into the coin slot. "I'll have to
give you two dollars and fifty cents; I just have quarters."

"If you should exceed three minutes," she said, "we'll
credit it to your call."

"Thank you." The last quarter fell into the machine with
a dull ring.

"Go ahead please."

"Beth," I said, reaching for my beer, "hello."

There was a long silence.

"Beth?"

"Hello?"

"It's Roger Hart."

A man stopped just outside the booth to blow his nose.

"Where are you." Beth said.

"Can't you hear?"

The man pushed his handkerchief into his pocket and
moved on.

"I'm at a dog track. I had some good luck with a dog."

"Dog racing?"

"The first time I've been," I said.

"Is that what you called to tell me?"

"No," I said, picking up the beer again, "it isn't." I glanced
up and noticed a sign on the wall beside the phone. "Wait a
minute," I said. "There's a sign that says the phones are disconnected a minute before post time."

"What's post time."

I read the sign again. "I wonder why that is."

"What's post time."

Still looking up at the sign, I rested the cup of beer back on the shelf; it was a narrow shelf, and as I removed my hand the cup tumbled off the edge, splashing beer across the front of my pants. I jumped up, banging my shoulder and the side of my head against the wall of the booth.

"Hello?" Beth said.

Beer had splashed onto the receiver of the phone. I shook it off and took it in my other hand and held it up to my face again. "My beer spilled."

"What?"

"It spilled." I reached down to lift up a sopping flap of my suit jacket. "Look at this."

"Hello?"

"One of those big cups." I turned around and looked down at the seat. There were only a few drops on it. I rubbed them off with my hand and sat down again. "One of those half-quart cups," I said, reaching down for the cup on the floor. "Nearly full."

"These things happen," Beth said.

"It's not your fault." I glanced at some beer running down the glass on the door. "Beth?"

"Yes?"

"Did you meet Mr. Becker when you were here last year? My boss at the travel agency?"

"No."

"He had a heart attack today over in Ceylon."

"Oh?"

"I've felt like telling someone since I heard — that was one reason for the call." I lifted up the end of my tie. It was soaked with beer. "He'll pull through all right, but it's got to me. We've gotten quite close." The cold beer had soaked through my suit and my underwear. "His wife called me from Ceylon."

"I'm really sorry."

I moved forward on the seat. "Beth," I said, "did you get my letter."

"Which one."

"The one on the personalized stationery."

"Oh yes," she said, "I got it day before yesterday."

I pushed my hand into my pants under my belt and held the wet cloth up from one of my thighs.

"I thought the letterhead came out very nicely," she said.

"Well Beth," I said, "I didn't mention anything in it about your proposal." I stood up again so the cloth wouldn't press down my legs. "I was sort of caught by surprise; I didn't know just what to say."

"Roger?"

"So I didn't say anything, but that was just because I didn't know the right way to say it." I removed my hand from my pants to pull the cloth out from my legs.

"Roger?" she said, "could you destroy that letter please?"

"What is it?"

"I regretted very much sending it," she said.

"You shouldn't have."

"It was right during the Spring Festival," she said. "Things were going very badly and that was one reason I wrote it."

A man stopped outside the phone booth and looked in at me. He had a dime in his hand. "Beth?"

"I think we should just be friends like before," she said. "Just correspondents. If I ever get to Boston again maybe we could have a reunion, but I think the other was a result of the pressure of the Spring Festival."

The man moved on to the next booth.

"Beth," I said, "I need a change in my life."

A new voice sounded in the receiver, the voice of an operator. "It's two minutes till post time," she said. "In one minute the phones will be disconnected."

"Why."

"Roger?"

"Beth listen."

"What's post time."

The man with the dime came back in front of the door. He motioned for me to hang up, then cupped his hand beside his mouth. "I got to make a call."

I turned to the side. "Beth, we have less than a minute to talk before the dog race."

"I told Nell my idea of getting married," Beth said, "Aunt Nell?"

"Yes?"

"She cried on the phone when I told her. She said ever since I was a little girl it's been her dream for me to be a nurse and if I didn't get my degree she didn't know how she'd go on."

The man started tapping against the glass of the phone booth. "She's been supporting you, right?"

"Paying my tuition."

"We can pay her back," I said. "Over a course of a few years."

"It's not the money with her — it's the dream of healing."

I turned toward the glass again and motioned the man to go on. "Beth," I said, "I'm ready for marriage."

There was a silence.

"I couldn't handle the Spring Festival and the studies, too," she said. "You should have seen me."

"Beth?"

"Going crazy," she said. "Trying to make papier-mâché

flags one minute, then running off to the library to cram for a test the next."

"Beth, I want to marry you. I want to accept your proposal."

"No, Roger."

I glanced out to see the man with a dime walking away and shaking his head. He looked back over his shoulder at the booths and said something, then continued on.

"Escapism, Roger; that's all it would be for me."

"No Beth."

"It would though."

"Beth?" I squeezed the receiver more tightly in my hand. "Please Beth. Change your mind."

"I'm finished with that period in my life," she said. "I'll write you a letter about it."

The operator's voice interrupted again. "It is now one minute to post time. The phones are being disconnected."

"Beth!"

"What is post time anyway."

The phone went dead.

For a while I continued sitting with the receiver pressed against my ear, looking ahead of me at the dial of the phone. Then, out of the side of my eye, I noticed people moving on the other side of the glass. I turned my head. They were getting up from the benches and starting toward the track. A man passed by, tucking a program into his pocket. Another one passed by, lighting a cigar. The man with the white sack on his lap passed by the other side of the glass eating a white doughnut. Slowly I returned the receiver to its hook and sat watching the people move back toward the track. The music stopped. "Thirty seconds till post time." The crowd began moving past the glass slightly faster. The music started again.

A few people remained sitting on the benches. I watched one at the other side of the room who was bent forward and rummaging around in a paper box beside his bench. The music stopped again. "It is now post time," the voice said. "And there goes Swifty!"

Rick had been standing over by the refreshment stand but I hadn't seen him since he was nearly concealed behind a large transparent bulb with orange juice streaming down its sides. He bent sideways to spit, and as he was straightening up he noticed me in the booth. He looked at me a moment, then started over, reaching into his pocket for a cigarette and lighting it as he walked. I pushed the door open as he approached. "Get cut off?" he said.

"Yes."

"They cut you off a minute before the races start," he said. "That's so you can't call out the results to bookies."

"Oh."

He spit again. "Amazing what some people'll do to make a buck." He looked in at me and at my pants. "What happened."

"I spilled some beer on myself." I looked down at the empty cup. "I was making a call; it sort of teetered off the shelf."

"You want this?" he said, removing a handkerchief from his back pocket.

"It's okay."

He returned the handkerchief to his pants. "You bet on Harry's Hero?"

"I didn't bet on this race. I thought of a person I wanted to call instead."

He took a deep drag on his cigarette. I looked up at him, then over his shoulder. Way on the other side of the room, past all the benches and leaning against one of the concrete supports was the girl he had pointed out before. She was filing her nails. "So," he said.

"So."

"Can I buy you another beer?"

"No, thanks."

It was quiet again. He held the cigarette up in front of his face and looked at the ash. He flicked off part of it with the finger of his other hand. "You was looking back at Joanna."

"I noticed her back there."

He stepped aside and motioned back toward her with his head. "Come on back and meet her."

I looked at my watch.

"Just say hello, that's all."

I got up off the seat and stepped out of the booth.

"Long as you don't have a dog this time." He started walking back toward her. "Good thing you didn't take Harry's Hero after all; I found out at the last minute he has the flu."

He walked along beside the benches, scuffling through newspapers on the ground, and I followed him. Joanna was leaning with her back against the concrete beam, holding her nails up very close to her face and concentrating on them as she filed them. "Joanna?" Rick said as we got closer. She filed a moment longer, then looked up. "I want you to meet a good friend of mine. Roger." He turned to me.

"They call me Roger."

He looked back at Joanna. "They call him Roger."

"Hi," I said.

"My pleasure." She began filing again.

"I was telling Roger earlier on; you was noticing him as he came in through the gates."

She didn't look up from her nails.

No one moved for a moment, then Rick reached out for the end of my tie. "He spilled some beer on himself in the phone booth." He turned the end of it over. "I hope this won't run."

"No."

Joanna lowered her nail file and looked down at my jacket and pants. "Beer?"

"It fell off the shelf."

"One of those big cups?" she said.

I held one of my hands about a foot above the other. "It was."

"Full?"

"Nearly."

She shuddered slightly. "Must have been cold."

"It was when it soaked through."

Rick put his hand on my arm. "Roger, I see my brother over there. I'll be right back." He turned and hurried off, disappearing around a corner.

Joanna began filing her nails again. "I once spilled scalding coffee on myself," she said.

"Painful."

She transferred the file to her other hand and began filing the nails of the hand that had been holding the file before. "I'll never forget it." A shiny black purse was resting on the floor beside her. "Shall we go over to my place?" she said, bending down to pick it up.

"I don't know."

"It's close."

I looked down at one of my shoes. "Actually I wanted to see another race or two."

"You can get back in." She opened the purse and dropped the file into it. "They stamp the back of your hand as you go out, then you show them when you want to come back in."

I reached into the side pocket of my coat for the program. "Let's see how many more races there are."

"They go till one o'clock." She took my other hand and began leading me. "I'll show you where you get your hand stamped. It's weird. Ultra-violet. You can't see nothing, then you put your hand under this special lamp and it comes out creepy purple."

We walked past several more concrete supports and a newsstand. Over at the side of the turnstiles was a gate with a man standing beside it. As we approached he reached down for a stamp on a shelf and stamped it down a few times on an ink pad. Joanna smiled at him. "Stamp us, Moe." She went first and held out her hand. He took it in one of his and stamped the back of it. I went next and held mine out. He took it and stamped it. I walked out after Joanna. She pointed across the parking lot. "See that house, that brown one?" There was a row of brown houses on the other side of the lot.

"Oh yes."

"That's where we're going."

We walked up to the street and she took my hand again. We stepped out into the street, waited while a car passed, then crossed. The man sitting on his chair at the entrance of the parking lot was reading a comic book. We walked past him and started past the rows of cars. "You like the dog races?" she said.

"I've never been before. Yes, I do."

"They're fun." We turned down one of the aisles. "If you win especially."

"I won in the first race."

Joanna stopped a moment and opened her purse. She reached inside for a package of gum, then she pulled one of the pieces out slightly and held it out to me.

"I don't."

She pushed it toward me. "Come on. Keeps your teeth clean."

I reached down and removed the stick of gum.

She took one for herself and then dropped the package back into her purse and snapped it closed and we started walking again.

"It's no fun when you lose," she said, pulling off the gum wrapper and dropping it on the ground. "You know what I mean?"

"Actually I haven't lost yet." I removed my wrapper, crumpled it up and put it into the side pocket of my coat.

"When you win," she said, sticking the gum into her mouth, "it's great. There's nothing like winning. But when you lose . . ." She shook her head. "I don't know what there is about it, but I don't like it."

I put the piece of gum in my mouth and started chewing on it. "I think I know what you mean."

"It leaves an empty feeling."

"Losing."

"I mean you give your money, you go down to the fence, you watch the race, and that's it. Nothing." She turned and we started walking between cars again and toward the back of the lot. "But winning is different. You pay your money, you go down to the fence, you watch the dogs run, your dog wins, you jump up and down. I mean it's just different, you know what I mean?"

"I think I do."

"I mean it's hard to explain. I can't explain it."

"You did explain it."

"Just different," she said. "That's the only way I know how to put it."

"I'm sure it is."

We walked between some more cars and then approached the far edge of the parking lot. "You have to go through some bushes," she said. "There's a trail through them."

We walked across some dirt, then there were some trees. There was grass on the ground and bushes but a dirt trail led through them. "We could have gone clear around," she said, "but I didn't think you'd mind going this way."

"I don't."

She went first, still holding my hand, and I followed, chewing the gum. On the other side of the trees was a wooden apartment house. A clothesline stretched out across its backyard with three sheets and a black slip hanging from the line. "Through here," she said, leading me along beside the building.

In the street was a boy with a stick and another boy throwing a rubber ball to him. The boy with the stick swung at it and missed, then turned around and chased the ball. "In here." She turned and we walked across the front yard. There were some patches of green grass in it but mostly it was dirt. We walked up the wooden steps and onto the front porch.

On the edge of the porch on a wooden rocking chair was an old man. He looked over at me, then held his hand out over the side of the porch. "Look's like rain," he said.

"Could be," I said.

There was a heavy door leading into the building with a large glass window in the top half of it. Joanna pushed it open and we went through. "Second floor," she said. Still holding hands, we walked up the wooden stairs. At the top she opened her purse and reached in for a key. We walked a few steps down the hallway and stopped at a door. She inserted the key into its lock, then pushed it open. "Go on."

I walked in ahead.

There was an old couch against the wall but nothing else in the living room. She walked across the floor to a door, opened it and went through. I followed her. She turned on a

light. There was a bed in the room with four tall wooden
bedposts and the shades were drawn. She set her purse
down on a table, then sat on the edge of the bed. "So," she
said, "your name's Roger."

"That's correct."

She looked down at one of my knees. "I knew a Roger
once. I mean I didn't know him well, but I knew him."

"It's sort of a semi-common name," I said.

She looked back up at my face. "It is, yes."

I put my hands in my pockets.

Joanna reached down and took off one of her shoes. She
brought it up and held it in her lap. It was quiet for quite a
long time except for the two boys in the street yelling at each
other. "I might as well tell you," she said, "usually when they
come up here they're sort of drunk. Passionate. I have to
sort of fight them off usually."

"I see," I said, removing my hands from my pockets.

"Not that I'm being critical."

"Probably I'd be drunker if I hadn't spilled the beer in the
phone booth."

She nodded.

"I'm sure I would be."

I glanced over at one of the shades. It had been pulled
down almost to the bottom, but not quite, so there was a
line of gray light coming underneath. Outside was a me-
tallic thump as though a ball had landed on the top of a car.
One of the boys laughed.

"I guess I'll take off my other shoe," Joanna said. After
waiting a moment she bent forward and removed the other
shoe and held it in her lap with the first.

"Passionate," I said.

"Excuse me?"

"You said they're usually passionate."

"They tend to be," she said. "Yes."

I looked over at a chair in the corner. "I think I'd be more passionate," I said, "except for this phone call I just had. May I sit down?"

A stocking was hanging on one of the arms of the chair. "Let me get that." Joanna got up and walked over to remove the stocking.

"This phone call," I said, walking to the chair. "I think that's sort of behind my feelings."

"Shall we get in bed and talk?"

I seated myself on the chair. "This girl Beth. She's a nursing student out in Wisconsin."

Joanna rolled the stocking around one of her fingers.

"I mean I don't want to bore you . . ."

"No."

". . . but if I could sort out my feelings about things . . ."

"Sure."

I crossed my legs and bent forward. "Another thing: my boss had a heart attack today."

"Oh?"

I uncrossed my legs. "Things are piling up; that's what I'm trying to say."

"Here." Joanna was holding out her hand.

I looked up at it a moment, then reached out and took it. She helped me back up from the chair.

"Then there's this girl Melinda. In a way she's really the one."

"Can I give you a back massage."

"It probably wouldn't help too much," I said. "You can try."

She put her hands under my coat and up under my arms and on my shoulders and began to squeeze the muscles.

"The thing is," I said, "I was in the Coast Guard for two years, just a desk job. Before that I was kind of unstable. Then after I got out of the service I decided the most important thing was to be stable; nothing else really mattered."

"Come to the bed." Keeping her arms up under my arms, she began moving me across the floor toward the bed.

"Do you know what I mean at all."

"Stable."

"I mean I was never really all that wild. I hitchhiked across the country once, doing odd jobs." We had reached the edge of the bed. "That was the most unstable time in my life."

"Sit." She helped me down onto the edge of the bed.

"I went to Bowdoin," I said. "You probably haven't heard of it."

"I don't know too many colleges."

"That's where I'm from, up in Maine."

"Can we take off the coat?"

"Yes."

She unbuttoned my coat and began removing it.

"But I never finished," I said, removing one arm from a sleeve. "There was a girl named Ellen. We just started off, hitchhiking. She lived there in the town where the college was. She kept asking me to just start off with her and then one day I did."

"Can you lie on your back?"

"Yes I can."

I lay down on my back and brought my legs onto the bed. "It was spring so we slept out at first. In forests, meadows, all over."

Joanna loosened my tie and removed it from my collar and then began unbuttoning my shirt. "We got out as far as Kansas. Then we were eating dinner in a diner one night and a man came over and sat down next to her. I was on one stool and she was on the next and the man sat down on the next one and said, 'Let's go,' to her. That's all he said. I mean he looked at her for a while and then he said, 'Let's go.' So she did. They got down from the stools and went out and got in a pickup truck and left. I watched in the mirror as they drove away."

"That's sad," Joanna said. She was unbuckling my belt. "It was."

She finished unbuckling the belt and then unzipped the fly and brought the pants down around my knees. Then she started untying one of my shoes.

"It was sad I didn't do anything about it but just sit there. But I mean it wasn't completely unexpected. Things had already gotten strained between us. She might even have winked at the guy to make him come over, I don't know. I'm sure he sensed there was something strained between us."

She pulled off one of my shoes and let it clunk to the floor. "Sad."

"In any case he said, 'Let's go,' and they went out and drove away and that's the last I ever saw of her. I mean we had plans to get married, but then we went on the trip and this empty feeling came between us and there didn't seem any way to get over it."

She untied the other shoe and dropped it on the floor.

"Maybe I should stop talking."

"If it helps you . . ."

"I've never told anyone about that time in the diner."

She pulled my pants down over my feet and draped them across the foot of the bed. "If it's too painful . . ."

"It's just that I didn't act manly. I mean I should have hit the guy. Afterwards I kept thinking of how I could have spun around on my stool and knocked him out. The only thing was, I knew if he left with Ellen I'd be free to forget the trip and go back home again."

She rolled one of my socks off my foot, then the other. Then she helped me up slightly and removed my shirt. "Long trips can really get monotonous," she said. She eased me down again and draped the shirt over the end of the bed.

"Then what," I said. "Oh yes. I got a job with the Kansas Department of Highways where I walked along the side of the road with a box putting in trash; but that was just for a day."

I was naked. Joanna knelt beside me on the bed. "Shall I take my things off?"

"Fine."

She reached down to her side and unfastened the clasp of her skirt.

"I got a couple other of these jobs. I felt I should be having the experience of them but my heart wasn't really in it. Dishwashing at one place. Just as I worked my way back to the East. Trying to think things out as I went along."

She unwrapped the skirt from around her waist and dropped it on the floor.

"So I got back," I said. "September? No, October. I got back to Maine in October and went up to college again. I went up there and went and saw the dean. He was a good person." I brought my hands up and put them behind my head. "I mean I leveled with him. I've had a spree, I said, a binge. I don't know if it could happen again, but I want to ask your advice. I'll respect it."

Joanna pushed her slip and underwear down her legs and over her knees, then removed them and let them fall on the floor.

"It was the first real talk I'd had with him. I mean I'd met him before, freshman orientation week, but not to get to know him. We must have talked three or four hours. Really nice guy."

"He sounds nice."

"You couldn't help liking him."

"That's quite a story," Joanna said, reaching up behind her neck and then pulling her sweater up over her head.

"I won't go into the whole conversation between myself and the dean, although in many ways it represented a turning point in my life. Just to communicate with another individual the way I did with him."

She dropped the sweater on the floor.

"The upshot was, though, that he said I was welcome back any time but that his personal opinion was that if I got my military obligation out of the way at that time, then I'd probably come back and feel more settled. So that's how I happened to wind up in the Coast Guard for two years." I cleared my throat. "As far as choosing the Coast Guard over the other branches was concerned, that was mainly due to my background. We lived on the coast. My grandfather had one of these whaling fleets. Excuse me, I mean my great-grandfather. My grandfather was also in fishing, lobstering, but the big whaling fleets had pretty much gone out by his time. My father has a contracting company but we've always had a ketch there in the harbor and gone out on weekends ever since I can remember."

"What was your name?" Joanna said.

"Roger."

Joanna looked down at me for a few moments, then lifted one of her knees and placed it between my legs. She reached behind her back and unfastened the straps of her bra, then removed it and let it fall to the floor. She brought her hands back in front of her and cupped them under her breasts. "Hi, Roger."

"Hi," I said. "Actually, it was the dean who got me the job with the travel agency. I went back and finished up college after the Coast Guard and he learned about this job for me. There was an accounting job or this one and I decided I'd feel more useful helping people plan their travel."

"Do you like these?" Joanna said.

"What's that."

She raised her breasts up slightly in her hands.

"Oh. Yes."

"I've had many people say they're the nicest ones they've ever seen."

"They're very nice."

"Can you sit up?"

I looked at her a moment, then raised myself up to my elbows. She bent forward and moved one of her breasts against my face. It covered my nose and mouth but by opening my mouth and moving my lower jaw backward I could still breathe. She put her arms behind me and eased me back down. "Now," she said, "were you saying something?" She kissed my cheek.

"What was I saying."

"Shhhh."

"Oh," I said. "It was during this period, first of working my way back from Kansas after the trip, them of being in the Coast Guard two years, then of going back to finish up college, that I decided that the most important thing in life was to be stable, to have a stable feeling." I felt her hand moving down over my chest and across my stomach and along one of my thighs. "Not that I was ever one of these really mixed-up people you hear about; I wasn't."

Her hand had moved between my legs. "What about this," she said softly.

"What's that."

"We can't really do anything with it like this, can we?"

"I don't want to seem personal," I said, "but I think this is the best talk, just a straightforward talk, that I've had since that afternoon in the dean's office."

She bent her mouth close to my head. "Can we do something about this down here?"

"Right." I removed one of my hands from behind my head and rested it on her side, then brought it around and held one of her breasts.

"There it comes; much better."

"You know something?"

She lifted her knee up and moved my legs together, then put her knee down on the bed again so that she was straddling me. "Now."

"You know something?"

"Know what."

"I've had this goal, to become stable, I've had it for several years now, in my mind all the time, but I've never really told anyone about it, not that it's really that exciting to hear, but I've never mentioned it before; but it's the one thing that's the most important thing to me. In a way it's what keeps me going."

"Shall I go ahead?" She moved forward up across my legs.

"But of course it has its boring side, stability."

She was pushing one of her hands down between us. "I'm going to go ahead, Roger."

"On the one hand I don't have a feeling of fear, like some people must have. I'll get enough money at the end of the week; food, a place to live. I don't have to worry about these things, or even think about them, which is good."

"You're in," she said, "all right?"

I nodded.

She began moving slowly up and down over me.

"But on the other hand," I said, "I sometimes get the feeling that there has to be something more, you know? In addition to. I mean I wouldn't want to give up the money and the food and the place to sleep. But sometimes I get the feeling that people who settle for this, people who have this as their goal, that it's just not enough. Do you get this feeling?"

Her hands were squeezing my sides as she moved up and down. Her eyes were tightly closed.

"Do you?"

She groaned but didn't answer. Her breasts hung down and swung forward and backward as she moved.

"I've thought of marriage, of course, but I don't think this would solve it. It's what everyone does, and I hope I don't sound like I'm trying to be superior to other people but I really don't think the things you see everyone trying to attain are really that great. They're nice. To eat enough and have money come at the end of the week is nice; you need these things. But the thing I'm finding out there's something very boring about them in themselves, not that you don't need them, you do."

Joanna opened her mouth and began sucking air in. "Oh God," she said. "Oh God!"

"But I don't know what the next step is. I've gotten this secure feeling, this stable feeling, and now there's a next step. But I don't see what it is yet. Something different, but without giving up this stable feeling that I've gone about getting for myself."

"Oh God." She collapsed down on top of me, crushing her breasts against my chest. Her mouth fell open against my shoulder and I could feel the moisture as she breathed heavily against my skin.

"My parents were always worried about money," I said. "I

mean not really worried, not bickering or anything, but I don't think they ever felt really free to think about other things as much as they would have liked. Everything they thought of doing wasn't quite as much fun as it should have been because there was always the financial consideration to think of. I don't feel this way though. I'll always have enough money. I don't want to think about money. I don't think I have to. But my father, for instance." Joanna took several more deep breaths, then slowly slid off me and onto the bed again. She lay beside me, letting her hand rest on my chest. "Not that he wasn't generous. He was generous. He never held anything back from me that I needed. There was never any question, like you hear of in some families, of quarrels." Joanna moved off the bed and picked up her panties and bra and began putting them on. "I have no gripes about my upbringing. I have two younger sisters and I'm sure they have no gripes either. We never lacked. I'm not saying we were a rich family, we weren't." After putting on the bra and underpants Joanna wrapped her skirt around her and buttoned it, then pulled on her sweater again. She sat down on the bed and put on her shoes. "I'm sorry I've gotten so wound up," I said.

"It does good to talk."

I looked up at a corner of the ceiling. "I'd say we were a family with an average income."

"Can I put your things on for you?"

"That would be . . . thank you."

She picked up my shirt from the end of the bed, put her hand under my back and helped me up. She put on the shirt and buttoned it down the front. Then she took my pants and underpants and pulled them up over my legs.

"This isn't a bad place," I said, "I mean it's big."

"It's okay." She buckled my belt and zipped up my fly.

I tilted my head slightly. "What's that," I said.

"What's what." She picked up my socks and started working them onto my feet.

"That noise. Is it coming from the dog track?"

"It's the announcer," she said. "You can hear him all over."

"I just noticed it."

She finished putting on my socks, then picked up my shoes from the floor and put them on and tied them.

"I'll get my coat on," I said. I got up off the bed and picked up my coat and put it on. "Let's see now." I removed my wallet and opened it. I pulled out a twenty dollar bill and a ten dollar bill. "Here."

She took it. "Thank you."

I put the wallet back in my pocket. "Are you going back to the track?"

"I thought I would," she said. "Let me just go into the bathroom." She walked in through a door and closed it. I heard running water inside. Aside from the bed and the chair the only other piece of furniture in the room was a large wooden bureau with a mirror built into the top of it. I walked over to it and ran my hand across the top of my head to smooth my hair. In the center of the bureau was a black-and-white photograph in a plastic frame. One part of the frame was broken away. The picture was of a man standing on a dock somewhere with a huge fish suspended beside him on a crane and some pulleys. The fish had a long bill which was hanging down toward the dock. The man was smiling and holding a fishing pole in one hand while he rested the other hand on the fish. I looked at it for a few moments and then walked over to the window. I lifted up the shade. The boys weren't playing in the street anymore. It was nearly dark, but over another row of houses I could see the top of a

Ferris wheel and some seats at the end of steel poles that were part of another ride. None of them were moving. Beyond that was the sea and the gray horizon. I let the shade fall. There was the sound of a toilet being flushed, then the door opened again and Joanna came out. "Are you going back to the track?" she said.

"I might just see one more race," I said. "I don't feel like betting any more."

4

BETH CAME TO BOSTON a week later, on a Wednesday, between noon and one o'clock. I had just finished my lunch. I dropped the plastic fork back into the sack, crushed the paper cup that the coffee had come in and pushed it back into the sack. I moved out from the desk slightly and looked under it at the wastebasket. It was filled with papers. Several crumpled papers had spilled out onto the rug. I turned and tossed the paper bag at a wastebasket in the corner that was less full. The bag hit the rim, balanced for just an instant, then fell onto the floor. I swiveled back around in the chair and pulled myself up to the desk again and saw Beth.

She was across the street. She had a round plaid carrying case in one hand and a larger plaid suitcase in the other and was starting across the street. She stepped back as a taxi raced in front of her, then looked quickly both ways and hurried forward again, stopping as a bus went by, then stepping between two parked cars and up onto the sidewalk.

I rose slowly from my chair.

She glanced at the window, then started toward the door.

"Beth," I said. She came forward and walked into the travel agency. "Beth."

Her face was very white and on one side of her head some of her hair was sticking out over her ear.

"Beth?" I said, taking another step forward.

Suddenly her chin started to move and then she began to cry. "Put these down," I said, taking the carrying case to set on the floor. "Now."

She started shaking her head.

"Sit down, Beth." I helped her slowly across the carpet to a chair by my desk. She continued to cry. "You're in Boston," I said.

"I shouldn't be here."

On the seat of the chair was a brochure of Alaska showing a photograph of a totem pole. "Here," I said, helping her down onto it.

"I shouldn't."

"You're in Boston," I said. "I'll get you some water." I hurried into the back room and turned on the tap and held a cup under it. When it was full I carried it back into the other room. She had put her face down on her arms on the desk. "Water," I said.

"I don't want it."

Several boys had stopped on the sidewalk and were looking in at us. I walked over and pulled the doorstop out from under the door and closed the door, then returned to the desk. "When did you get here."

"This morning."

I went around for my swivel chair, pulled it beside Beth's chair and sat. "Did you just get here?"

"At two A.M."

"Did you fly?"

"Yes." She made a loud wet sniffing sound.

"From Wisconsin."

"Yes," she said, "I changed at Chicago." She started sobbing again.

"Your school," I said.

"I just left it."

"For good?"

"I don't know."

I pulled my chair up closer. "Have you eaten?"

"On the plane."

I got up from the chair. "I'll go get something."

"I couldn't eat," she said into her arms. "I don't know what's happening."

"A bowl of soup?"

"I couldn't."

I looked down at the top of her head a few moments, then sat down again. "You should eat."

"I'd be sick."

I rested my hand on the desk. "You haven't graduated."

"No."

"Did you tell people you were leaving?"

"I called them all from Chicago," she said. "Between planes. I called Nell and my parents and the school and told them all from the airport." She began shaking her head and crying again. "It was awful. The whole way I kept wishing the plane would crash."

I picked up the cup of water again. "Take a sip of this."

"When I told Aunt Nell . . ." Beth said. "I was in the phone booth and I told Aunt Nell I wasn't going to be a nurse anymore . . ."

I set the water down again. "What happened."

"She just . . . there was a long silence. I told her I'd left school and I wasn't going to be a nurse anymore and there was a long silence for a while and then she started making this sound."

"What sound."

"I don't know," Beth said. "It was like a whistling sound, only it wasn't like she was whistling like you do through your lips. It was like it was coming up from her throat, like a moaning sound. I just stood there in the phone booth listening to this sound come out of the phone. I kept asking her if she was all right. But she just kept making the sound and then she hung up."

"I'm sure she's all right."

Beth raised her head a few inches, then wiped one of her forearms across her eyes. "I'm so sorry to be doing this."

"Don't be."

She rubbed her other hand across her arm. "There's some Kleenex in my suitcase."

"Shall I get it?"

"I have to," she said, "it's locked." She got up from her chair, leaving a clean area in the dust on the top of the desk where her arms and face had been. She walked over to the suitcases and lifted up the hem of her dress. "That night you called," she said. "I was studying rashes." She turned up the hem of the dress. A small pocket with a button in the center of it had been sewn on the inner side of the material. She unbuttoned it and reached in for a very small key. "Skin rashes," she said, getting down on her knees in front of the suitcase. "Eczema. I was studying eczema just as Dorothy Ash, another girl on the floor, came in and told me there was a phone call." She inserted the key into a small lock on the handle of her carrying case and turned it, but it didn't come open. "So I got up and went down the hall to the phone and we had the talk."

She turned the key over and inserted it in the lock the other way. She turned it but still the small padlock didn't come open. "Then I got back to the room after the call and sat down and looked at the book, this picture of someone's leg with eczema on it, and I sort of had this horrible feeling like I knew I was never going to be a nurse."

I stepped up to her and bent over. "Let me try that."

She removed the key and handed it to me. I inserted it in the padlock and began jiggling it around and turning it.

"It just hit me. Really for the first time. It had been coming, I think, but after the call I just knew all of a sudden that I couldn't go on. Aunt Nell used to buy me little play nursing outfits when I was little. Everyone always said I was going to be one of the great nurses; they called me Florence Nightingale, joking, only they weren't really joking." I removed the key and turned it the other way and put it in again. "So I came back from the phone call and sat down. I tried to read on a little bit. Then I came to this paragraph that I knew I should have been underlining. It was about the appearance of the scaliness in a person with eczema. I picked up my underlining pencil because I knew it was something I should underline. But I couldn't. Just physically I couldn't underline it even though I knew it was something that was sure to be on the test the next day."

"Either this key is bent," I said, removing it from the padlock, "or it's not the right one."

"It's not the right one." She took it back and lifted up the hem of her dress and returned it into the small pocket and buttoned it. "I'm not thinking very well." She turned up the hem of her dress and returned it into the small pocket and hem again, where there was another pocket, this one sewn on at a slight angle. She unbuttoned it and reached in for another key, similar to the first one. "There was a book one of the girls had at school," she said, handing it to me. "It told all these handy hints for traveling. That's how I learned to sew these little pockets in."

I inserted the key in the padlock and turned it. It snapped open.

She pulled the zipper around in a circle, then opened the

flap of the suitcase and reached in for a box of Kleenex, squashed in the edge. She pulled out a violet sheet of it and blew her nose. "Is there a wastebasket?"

I pointed to the one against the wall.

Beth walked over and dropped the piece of Kleenex in the wastebasket. "The words on the page just stopped having meaning," she said. "I had the book in front of me and my notebook propped up against the wall. I looked up at the notes and they didn't have any meaning either."

"I think we can talk about all this in time," I said. "I'd like to ask you a few things though."

"Of course." She removed another violet tissue from the box to wipe her eyes.

"You got here early this morning."

After wiping her eyes she crumpled it and dropped it in the wastebasket. "Yes."

"Have you just been walking around since then?"

"I sat at the airport for a while, about four hours I guess, trying to decide whether to come here or not." She carried the Kleenex box back to her suitcase. "Then I got a taxi in here from the airport. I walked around some more, debating with myself." She zipped the top of the suitcase back up.

"But you haven't eaten."

"I didn't want to," she said, "because I can think better on an empty stomach."

I pointed down at the suitcases. "This is all the luggage you have."

"I have a foot locker and a trunk coming," she said. She tipped up the round carrying case and rested it beside the larger bag.

"Coming where."

"To here," she said. "The travel agency. It has my lamps in it and my blankets and pillow. I didn't know what else to do except put everything in and ship it here. I realize I probably shouldn't have."

"You should have."

Beth turned the hem of her skirt up and inserted the key into the pocket and buttoned the pocket's flap. "As soon as the things get here I'll have them taken right over to where I am at the time; I'll get them right out of your way." She straightened up and smoothed the front of her dress.

"Do you know anyone else in Boston?"

"No," she said. "There was a girl on the plane from Chicago who sat next to me. Very nice. She's here somewhere but I don't know where; she'd be the only other person I know."

I raised my arm up and looked at my watch. "Quarter of two," I said.

Beth gestured at the telephone on the desk. "If it wouldn't be an inconvenience," she said, "maybe I could call up someplace for some accommodations; that would probably be the next step for me."

"I have a hide-a-bed in the living room of my apartment."

She shook her head. "I couldn't."

I walked over and picked up the carrying case. "You're tired and hungry. If you get some food and some sleep I think we can talk about things. Right now I don't think either of us really know what to say." I bent down and picked up the other suitcase.

"I hate to think of myself as a burden."

"You're not a burden," I said. "I'm happy to see you."

"Are you?"

"Yes, Beth." I looked over at her a few moments, then put the suitcases down and walked over to her. I took her hands. "I mean I wouldn't have called you up if I didn't want to see you."

"You weren't drunk?"

"No."

"Because I've never done anything like this before."

"I know."

She walked back to her suitcases. She removed the key from her dress and got down on her knees. "Your letters," she said, putting the key in the padlock. "I don't know how many times I've read them over." She opened the padlock. "When I finally came to the point of deciding whether to come or not that's how I decided. I read them all through and decided to come." She pulled out a stack of letters with several rubber bands around it. "They're all here."

"I have yours in the apartment."

She pulled off the rubber bands. "You'll think I'm really stupid," she said, "but I even underlined certain parts of them." She opened the top envelope and removed the letter. "Not that they're great love letters but it's just the way you describe things; I wanted to read them over and over." She held out the letter in front of me. Halfway down the page, with a very straight line in red ink, there was a sentence that had been underlined. It read: "The window of the Volkswagen was accidentally left open last night so that during the big blizzard about a foot of snow was deposited on the seat of the car which I came out this morning to discover."

I read it, and nodded. "I'd forgotten about that."

"Just something about it. The way you put it or something." She folded the letter again, returned it to the envelope and put them back in the suitcase.

Then she stepped back and looked around the room. "You know, I can't really believe I'm here."

"You remember the office."

"Didn't you have different posters?" She was looking at a poster next to the door. It was a picture of the Taj Mahal but one of its corners had become unthumbtacked and was hanging down over part of the picture.

"We try and rotate posters every few months."

She looked at the wastebasket in the corner, then walked over and bent over and picked up a crumpled brown bag. She dropped it in the basket. "Was the janitor sick today?"

I picked up a piece of carbon paper up from the floor beside my shoe. "I'm trying to think," I said. "You say you haven't eaten but you aren't hungry."

"I don't feel hungry."

"Tired?"

"A little."

"What about this then. What about going over to my apartment and you sleeping for the rest of the afternoon; then when I come back, we could go out to dinner and talk."

She walked over to the swivel chair and sat down. "In a way," she said, "I'd like to talk now. Are you really busy?"

"Not really."

She swiveled around to look at me.

I pulled the other chair out from the desk again and sat down.

"If you have business on your mind," she said, "I don't want to bother you; it's just that I've been walking around thinking of these things I wanted to say."

"Go ahead."

She reached over to the desk and picked up a small plastic globe of the world. "This is nice."

"It's a paperweight."

"The reason I didn't come here at nine is that I had these things to say but I didn't know what they were. I just sort of came here, then I had to walk around this morning figuring out what to say." She turned the globe around to look at Asia.

"You're certainly welcome to say them."

"I mean it would be silly," she said, turning it a little more to look at the Pacific Ocean, "to just come in and say these things I'd memorized. That's what I was going to do at one point but I thought that would be awful."

I nodded.

"Don't you?"

"It would lack spontaneity."

"That's why I didn't come in at first. I didn't want to sound like a parrot." She put the paperweight back on the desk. "But the first thing," she said, reaching over to run her hand along the edges of the desk, "the most important thing, is that if you don't want me here I want you to say so."

"I do."

"But if you don't," she said, "I'd understand. That letter I wrote, asking you to marry me; I mean I've felt really terrible about it. I even went down to the post office and tried to get it back. It had sort of a pushy feeling to it and I hate that. So could you just tell me if you ever want me to leave?"

I nodded.

"Really."

"I will."

Suddenly there was a rustling around in another part of the room. We both looked over to see the poster of the Taj Mahal curling down along the wall. It curled itself up till it reached the two tacks holding in the bottom, then hung on the wall in a roll. "What happened," Beth said.

"The other tack came out at the top."

We continued looking over at it for a few more moments, then Beth got up from her chair. "I'm very serious," she said, "if you want me to go now, tell me."

"I will, Beth."

"Will you promise?"

"I promise."

She picked up the cardboard Eiffel Tower from the table. "What shall we do then," she said, "talk about marriage?"

"We could."

"This morning in the taxi coming in from the airport I thought maybe we could try an experimental situation for a while. I don't know what you'd think of that."

"What sort of situation."

She rubbed the front part of the tower with her finger. "I didn't really take it that far."

"Dating?"

She shrugged.

I got up and walked over to the filing cabinet, then ran my finger through a thick layer of dust on the top of it. "It seems sort of awkward to be talking about getting married before we know each other very well."

"Yes."

"Doesn't it?"

"It does."

I made another line through the dust. "You can only do so much with letters as far as getting acquainted."

"They're limited."

"We've sort of done all we can with letters," I said, making a line that cut through the first two lines, "wouldn't you say?"

"I would say that."

"Most people can sort of look back at things they've done together. Reminisce. We can't really reminisce about our letters very easily."

"We could," she said, setting the cardboard tower back on the table, "but I don't think it would be satisfying."

"We tried with the blizzard."

"I didn't think that was satisfying."

I shook my head. "It wasn't for me."

"No."

Beth set the Eiffel Tower back down on the table. "I bought these books," she said.

"What books are those."

Someone honked outside in the street.

"Nothing," Beth said.

"Books?"

She shook her head.

"Textbooks?"

"They're these books I bought in Wisconsin," she said. "During the Spring Festival, while I was getting ready for that, when I thought of us getting married. I bought them and studied up on them."

The end of my finger was covered with dust. I bent over to pick up a brochure that was on the floor and wiped the dust off on it. "What kind of books are they."

"It took me about five times walking past the store to get up the nerve," she said. "I mean I'd seen them in there before when I went in to get a dictionary. I hadn't opened them or looked at them, I'd just seen them."

I crumpled up the brochure. "I still don't . . ."

"They're in my bag." She turned around and pointed at the open suitcase.

"Do you want me to get them?"

She turned back the other way and reached up to smooth her finger across a tear in a poster on the wall. "At first I just felt awful about it. Disgusted with myself. I didn't even look at them till a week after getting them. I wanted to burn them but instead I stuck them in back of the closet behind all my roommate's shoe boxes."

I looked down at the suitcase.

"Then I started thinking about them and one evening I

stayed in my room during dinner and got one out and started reading it."

I glanced at Beth again, then at the suitcase.

"Just about a chapter or two, just during dinner, from six to six-thirty, while my roommate was gone. Then I got this disgusted feeling again and wanted to burn them but I didn't."

I set the crumpled brochure down on the corner of the desk and bent down over the suitcase.

"Then about four days later I stayed up in the room again during dinner and read some more. I mean I'd been thinking about them and wanting to read them and at the same time sort of hating myself, but then I read them again. The second time I read them I didn't feel so disgusted."

I pushed aside a blue bathrobe. Underneath were three books. I lifted them up out of the suitcase. "These?" She turned around to glance at them, but then looked back at the poster. Two of the books were paperback but brown wrapping paper had been glued over the covers. The other one was a hard-cover book and had a shiny maroon and white cover on it that said Thomasville Nursing School, then a circle in the center with a drawing of an outstretched hand and some Latin words around the drawing.

"I put the covers on the books so I wouldn't feel funny about reading them."

I sat down on the swivel chair with the books and opened one of the paper ones. At the top of the page a neat red line had been drawn under one of the sentences. It read, "If continued stimulation of this area fails to result in a heightening of passion, it would be best to desist, talk for a while, have a glass of water, then begin again with another technique."

"For most people," Beth said, "I guess these wouldn't be too shocking, but if you knew my family you'd realize why I feel so squeamish. It's just not the sort of thing you'd read in a million years if you were from my family."

I turned to a new page.

"But after I started doing the reading, after I got over the disgusted feeling I had at first, I realized that my attitudes, almost all of my attitudes on these matters, were completely wrong. I think most people's are."

About halfway down the new page was the heading "Intercourse During Pregnancy: some do's and don't's." The sentences under that had been heavily underlined in red.

"Not that it was anybody's fault," Beth said. "I just sort of grew up in the dark about these matters. I never thought about them. But after reading these books and studying them I realized it's important to think about them. They're as important as anything else. You can get real problems if you start thinking there's something about them that shouldn't be brought out in the open."

I turned to the front page of the book. It was *Marital Happiness Through Sexual Adjustment.* I set it on the desk and opened the next one.

Beth turned around. "But this society," she said, "I mean you can really see how they repress knowledge of this kind. How they actually make you feel guilty even to think about things of this kind."

I nodded and looked down at the book. The underlining was in blue pen.

"You can't blame anybody," Beth said. "It's just the way we are. But the Victorianism! I never realized it."

"It's bad." I turned a page.

"The unhappiness," she said. "Just because people are afraid to express themselves. Afraid of their own bodies. Feeling there's something bad about them; unclean. They're ashamed of their own natural processes. As though they were *un*natural." She stepped forward. "Let me see this one." She took from me the hardbound book and opened it. "Let me just read something." She began thumbing through. "It's near the front." She opened it to the front again, went through a few pages, then stopped. "Here." She cleared her throat. "They had these two groups. In a high school in a slum area in Chicago." She looked down at the book. " 'In Group A' — this was the group that was given sex education and training — 'in group A the marriage rate was eighty-two percent. The divorce rate was only twelve percent.' " She turned to the next page. "Listen to this." She cleared her throat. "This is the group that didn't have the sex education and training." Her voice lifted slightly. " 'In Group B the marriage rate was only forty-six percent and fully half of these were either divorced or separated by age thirty. By age thirty-five sixty-one percent were divorced or separated.' "

"They're for sex education."

She held up her hand. "Listen to this — 'In addition, Group B furnished society with two homosexuals, one prostitute and three rapists, who, at this writing, are serving life sentences in an Illinois state penetentiary.' " She handed the book back. I looked down at a graph on the page. "And people wonder why you have all the trouble. The frustration you have."

"We're an unenlightened people in many ways," I said.

Beth sat down on the chair beside me. "*I* was," she said. "I mean not that you should go out and have sex with the first person you see."

"No." I turned a page and looked at another graph with a steeply ascending line running across it.

"I've known people who went to that extreme too: a nursing student who had to leave school last month was one.

That's just as bad as the complete prudishness. It shows just as much a lack of awareness."

I glanced at the letters still resting on the edge of the desk. "There's a middle ground," I said.

"You have to be selective."

I took all three books, made a pile of them and set them back in the suitcase.

"But until I solve this problem," she said, "I don't really feel I can go on."

"What's that."

"This problem."

I tucked the bathrobe over the top of the books and straightened up in the chair again. "What problem is that."

"Of doing it," she said. "Of getting it done, so I don't have these myths in my mind."

"Doing . . ."

"I feel once I did it I could be much more realistic. Now it's like a big thing looming up. Even though I know it's not such a big deal, it's been on my mind. It must seem pushy for me to come here like this but if we could just do it I'm sure I could start thinking of other things again. I mean obviously I've never talked like this to another human being."

I looked down at the arm of my chair for a few more moments, then I got up. "You're talking about . . ."

"Yes."

I glanced down at the toe of one of my shoes. "I'll have to think a minute."

"Take your time."

It was quiet except for the traffic passing outside in the street. I put my hands in my pockets. "I agree there are a lot of myths around," I said. "Shall we go over to my apartment?"

Beth bent over and pushed the bathrobe aside and removed the books again. "Let me find something." She began thumbing through one of the books. "Where is that." She started thumbing through the next book. "There's a chapter that says it's best not to do it in a bed the first time."

"Why not."

She closed the book. "I can't find it."

"Why not do it in a bed."

"Because," she said, "it's best to do it in some setting that doesn't have any of the old romantic connotations. That way it helps to prevent some of the taboos from growing up around the act."

I nodded.

"So for that reason, if you don't mind, I'd just as soon not go to the apartment."

Beth bent forward to return the books to the suitcase. Then she straightened up, rested her hands on her legs and looked up at me. "Can we do it here?" she said.

"Where."

"Here," she said. "Maybe it wouldn't be possible; I don't know."

"In the office?"

She nodded, then got up from the chair, looked around the room and pointed over to the corner behind the filing cabinets. "What about there," she said. "Between the wall and that steel case."

I looked down at the rectangular shape of the carpet between the filing case and the wall. "Our heads would stick out." I gestured at the front window. "The people passing."

"What about this." Beth walked over to the cabinet, bent over and pulled out the bottom drawer. Then she pulled the next drawer up all the way out so that the space between the cabinet and the wall was extended. "Could they still see us?"

"No."

"I don't think they could." She reached down into the space between the cabinet and the wall and picked a paper clip up off the rug, then stepped back.

I walked to the corner and looked down into the rectangular space, then I looked at Beth, who was standing several feet away, holding the paper clip. The short sleeves of the yellow dress she was wearing were ruffled and there was a small fringe of white lace trim around them and around the neckline of the dress. I looked back down at the carpet. Outside in the street a car honked as it passed. "I wonder if I could ask you a question," I said.

"Of course." She set the paper clip in the ashtray on the desk. Then she stepped back to where she was.

I walked over to the chair and sat down again. "I don't really know what it is," I said. "I mean I have the feeling that there's something that's being left unsaid here." There was a pencil mark on one of the arms of the chair. I rubbed at it with my thumb.

"About safety precautions?" she said. "Because if you're worried about that, I'm not. If I have a baby, I have a baby. I want to."

I turned my thumb over and looked at it. It was gray. I rubbed it across the palm of my other hand. "You don't think there are things that need to be said then. Before going to the corner, if we do."

She shook her head, then bent over and scratched one of her knees. "I mean that's the whole thing. Not to say a lot of unnecessary things the way people do. Just go ahead and do it. Not waste time with talking but justify the urge. Be honest about it."

I nodded.

"That's the whole thing." She finished scratching her knee and straightened up again. She looked over at the corner.

"Do you smoke?" I said.

"Do I?"

"Yes."

"Why no."

I looked back down at the arm of the chair.

"Why."

"I don't know," I said.

"Do you?"

"No."

"I mean I've had a couple of cigarettes in my life. But I've never taken it up as a habit."

"I haven't either," I said, leaning back in the chair. "Do you drink?"

"Me? No."

"I don't either." I unfolded my hands and put them up behind my neck. "That night I called I'd had a beer. I think that was the first one I'd had in a month."

Beth walked over to the other chair and sat down. "I mean I've had drinks, I'm not saying that. I've gotten high. But I don't . . . it's not a habit." She looked down at the hem of her dress.

"Not that I would object to someone else doing it."

"No."

Beth put one of her hands down to the hem of her dress and took it between her thumb and forefinger. "It's their business."

"You haven't had . . . sexual experiences before."

"No," she said, not looking up, "oh no."

"I have."

She nodded. "I sort of . . ." She cleared her throat. "Being a boy . . . I imagined you had."

"Not to excess."

"No." She began rolling the hem back and forth between her thumb and forefinger.

"But in moderation I have."

She nodded. "Of course."

"So when you come in with the books and start telling me about it, reading me about it, telling me it's not good to do it in a bed . . ."

"I just said . . ."

"But you can see," I said, glancing over at her, then back down at one of my legs, "how I might . . ."

She put her other hand down next to her first hand and began rolling the hem of her dress between the thumb and forefinger of both hands.

". . . might be a little resentful."

"Oh."

"Not resentful. I'm not resentful. But you can see how . . ."

She put the hem back down and smoothed it. "It's just that I wanted to get rid of my misconceptions."

"I know that," I said. "That's fine. But coming in here with your suitcases, pulling out my file drawers and saying we'll do it over in the corner; you can understand that there might be some feelings of hesitancy on my part."

She shrugged.

"Can you?"

She reached over to the ashtray and removed the paper clip.

"This being my place of business," I said. "The place where I work."

"I don't think that should make so much difference."

"You don't."

"I think that's saying the sex act is some special thing, something that doesn't really have to do with our daily lives but rather has to be done in the darkness, in a guilty way."

I looked over at the filing cabinet again, then back at Beth.

"I think it's saying that I'm a travel agent. This is where I work."

She bent open the paper clip.

"You've come in here at one o'clock in the afternoon with this request. During my workday. And are you saying you don't see anything out of the ordinary about it?"

She bent the paper clip all the way out till it was a straight piece of wire.

"Are you?"

She shrugged again. "It might be out of the ordinary." She began bending the wire back into the shape of a paper clip.

I got up from the chair. "You've flown all the way back here just to see me. Is that correct?"

"Yes."

"Hoping we'll get married."

The length of wire was bent back to its original shape. "Not necessarily."

"In the letter you asked me if I wanted to marry you. Then in the phone call I asked you if you wanted to marry me. Do we want to get married?"

She returned the paper clip to the ashtray. "I don't know."

"I don't either. I thought at one point I did. It seemed like coming here, going back to the apartment in the evenings, having the weekends; it seemed like this wasn't enough. So I thought of marriage."

She nodded.

I looked down at the cardboard Eiffel Tower. "But then there's always the chance that it would be the same. There's always the chance that I'd come here, go back to the apartment in the evenings, have the weekends; but I'd be married. And it wouldn't be different at all. Maybe worse. What about that."

"I don't know."

I looked over at the handle of the door and at the lock below the handle. On the other side of the glass door a woman walked by carrying her purse. "Now you say you want to have sex over in the corner."

"Not if you don't."

"But you feel it would help you to do it that way. Help you to get over some misconceptions about things."

"Yes."

She took one of her thumbs in her other hand and looked at it.

"Isn't that it?"

"I don't know."

"Isn't it?" I said. "You've been studying up on it, and you want to put it into practice."

She nodded.

"I'm just trying to state the facts of the matter," I said, "because otherwise . . ." I walked over to the door and turned the lock underneath the handle. ". . . I mean ordinarily I wouldn't consider something like this. This time and place. What about our clothes."

She looked up.

"As far as leaving them on or taking them off," I said, walking over toward the corner, "since it's this romanticism we're trying to overcome I guess we should leave them on."

"Probably."

I looked down into the rectangular space. "So," I said, "what time is it now." I looked at my watch. "Nearly two. I have an itinerary to type up later; but that's all."

Beth was still sitting in the chair, looking down into her lap.

"And you're sure this is the way you want to do it," I said.

"I don't know." She shrugged. "Now I just feel pushy. I

feel like I've come in here and started telling you what to do.
I feel badly." She didn't look up from her lap.

"I wouldn't do it though if I didn't want to, you know."

"I feel aggressive now."

A tall man wearing a hat walked past the window. I
watched him pass. "I wonder if tall people could look down
behind the drawers." I walked to the front of the room and
moved the table away from the window. I stepped behind it
and stood up on my tiptoes. "It might be good to open all
three drawers," I said. "I think an extremely tall person
could look down over the second drawer." I walked back to
the filing cabinet and slid open its top drawer. "Could I say
something?"

"Yes."

"I *do* think there could be some value in doing it in the
corner."

Beth moved forward, then slowly rose from the chair. I
held out my hand and took hers.

"I mean I agree with you," I said, leading her over to the
corner. "I felt the way you presented it, with the books, the
underlining . . . I felt that wasn't very personal. But your
basic thoughts — I agree with them." Holding hands, we
stood looking down at the beige carpet between the wall and
the filing cabinet. "Do you want to get in first?"

"All right."

"We could lie this way," I said, gesturing into the space.
"Our heads up at this end."

"I'll take off my underwear." She reached up under her
dress and began pulling her underpants down over her legs.

I turned around and walked back to the desk, lifted the
receiver of the phone up off the cradle and set it down on the
blotter, then walked back to the filing cabinet. Beth eased
herself down onto her back and I stepped in beside her, then

got down on my knees and unbuckled my belt. "Those
books," I said. "Let's throw them out later. All that about
caressing the erogenous zones — shall we throw them out?"
   "If you think they've served their purpose."
   "I do."

5

THE FIRST TIME I saw Melinda again, or thought I saw her, was the Sunday after Beth had come to Boston. It was between nine and ten in the morning and Beth and I had walked down from the apartment to buy a newspaper. At the far corner of the Common is a subway entrance, then a structure where a wide flight of stairs leads down to the subway tracks. At the top of the stairs is a small newsstand with a newsman standing beside it. It was just after I had paid him for a newspaper that I thought I saw her. Beth bent down and picked up one of the papers off a stack on the ground. The man gave me change, and as I put it into my pocket my head turned, and I looked down the stairs and into the subway station below. Just as I was looking down into it Melinda, or a girl who I thought was Melinda, was passing through the turnstile. Two women and a boy went through after her, then she was gone. I turned to Beth, who was standing beside me with the newspaper under her arm. "I just saw Melinda," I said.

"Who?"

"That girl in the store. I just saw her going through the turnstile."

We both stood looking down the stairs ino the subway station.

"I'm not sure it was her," I said. "The hair." I removed the sports section. "Do you read the sports?"

"No."

"I usually throw away the sports and the classifieds so it's not so heavy to carry back." I walked around the side of the building to a litter basket. "You have to look through the classifieds." I opened the classifieds up at several places and looked inside. "Sometimes they continue the news of the week in the classifieds. Once I threw them out and had to come all the way back." I dropped the two sections into the wire basket.

"How was she wearing her hair," Beth said.

"Up on top of her head." We started back toward the apartment. "In the store it was hanging down straight."

We walked along a concrete path past benches where old men were sitting. We passed one holding a magazine up in front of his face and reading it. A few benches farther on, on the other side of the path, an old man was hunched forward, sleeping, his legs crossed. On a limb hanging out above our heads a squirrel ran along, stopped, then turned around and ran back the other way. "This used to be a cow pasture," I said.

"What did."

"This common," I said. I gestured off toward the street. "I've seen pictures of it. Paintings. Cows all in there. Grazing. If you're interested in historical things it's interesting."

We walked out to the street and down the sidewalk to my apartment, then turned up the walk and up the stairs and inside. We walked up the flight of stairs to my apartment, then I reached into my pocket and removed the key as we walked down the hall, opening the door at the end. I walked in and set the newspaper down on the couch. "What was the name of the hotel where she stayed before?" Beth said.

"Who."

"Melinda." She walked over to the couch and sat down next to the newspaper. "You said there was a hotel where you went up and there was the other person with her."

"The one near my office."

Beth removed the front section from the paper. "Maybe you could call and see if she's staying there."

I looked over at the phone. "I wonder."

Beth removed the next section of the paper, opened it, then pulled out a magazine section, looked at the front and pulled out another magazine section.

"Maybe I'll just call over there," I said. I walked over to the phone.

"This is too much news for one day," Beth said, looking down at the front of the second magazine section. She pulled out another part. "This much news at once is depressing."

There was a telephone book on the table next to the phone. I thumbed through it till I came to the *s*'s, then found Statler Hilton.

"It's depressing to go along day by day with a normal amount, and then this." She pulled out another section.

I dialed the number given after the name of the hotel. It rang once, then was answered. "Statler Hilton Hotel."

"I wonder if you could see if there's a Melinda Gray staying there."

"One moment." I looked back over at Beth. The different sections of the paper were spread out beside her on the couch and one section, the front section was on her lap. "What's news," I said.

"I'm just looking at the headlines."

There was a click in the receiver of the phone, then the woman came on again. "Can you hold a moment, sir?"

"I'll hold."

"It's funny," Beth said, looking down at the bottom of the page, "there are some things I never read. China. I never read about China for some reason."

"I don't either."

She looked up. "Really."

"I don't," I said. "I'll read about Japan, but I'll never read about China."

She looked back down at the page.

"I don't know why," I said. "I'll read about Africa; but I'll never read about South America."

"I'm the opposite."

"Really."

She looked over to another part of the page. "The Sahara," she said, "that's really about the only place in Africa that interests me. But South America. The governments down there."

"They interest you."

She nodded.

"Interesting."

Beth set the front section down beside her and pulled another one up onto her lap. "Of course gardening," she said. "I can never read the gardening section."

"I can't."

There was another click on the phone. "Sir?" the girl said.

"Still here."

"I'm sorry; we have no one by that name registered here."

"Thank you." I hung up the phone.

Beth looked up from the paper. "No?"

"She's not there," I said, walking over toward the couch. "I really think it was someone else; the different hairdo." I seated myself on the end of the couch. I picked up a magazine section and looked at its cover. Then I set it down and moved the first section onto my lap. Toward the bottom was the headline "Thousands Believed Dead in South China Flood." "Wait a minute," I said. "I'll have to take back what I said."

"What's that."

"Never reading about China."

Beth was looking at a black-and-white picture of a rose-bush on the front of her section. "You do then," she said.

"The political things I don't. I never read about the revolutions or the leaders over there. But something like this . . ." I pointed to the headline.

Beth glanced over at it, then back at the rosebush. "You read that," she said.

"I don't know why," I said. "Floods, earthquakes, mine disasters. Any natural disasters. Always." I looked down under the headline and started to read. " 'For eight days rampaging flood waters have ravaged southern China, destroying entire villages, leaving tens of thousands homeless and at least one thousand dead.' " I glanced over at Beth, who was reading the article under the picture of the rosebush. "I thought you didn't read gardening news."

"I don't usually," she said. "This is a new way of killing aphids. You attract them sexually, then kill them."

"Oh?"

"I'm just reading it."

I watched her reading for a few moments, then looked back at the article on the rampaging floods.

The next time I saw Melinda I was trying on a summer suit on the second floor of a clothing store two blocks down from the travel agency. It was in the afternoon. I had passed by the window several times and noticed a light blue suit that was on sale, then finally I decided to go up and try it on.

It was about two o'clock when I went in. A man came forward, smiling, and I indicated the suit in the window and said I would like to try it on. Continuing to smile, he removed a measuring tape from his pocket and measured my arms and legs, then returned the tape and walked over to a rack. He removed a light blue suit from the rack and handed it to me. There were two dressing rooms at the side of the room. He bent over slightly and glanced under the doors, then told me I would have to go to the dressing room at the top of the stairs. I thanked him and carried it to the stairs and up. At the top I pushed open a door and went inside. There was a wooden chair inside and a small dusty window at eye level that looked out over the street.

Standing in my socks, I finished tucking my shirt in around the top of the pants. I buttoned the middle button of the jacket, then extended my arm out to see where the end of the sleeve came to on my wrist. The direction that I extended my arm was toward the window. As I was looking at the end of the sleeve, my eyes slowly changed their focus, till I was looking through the small dusty pane of glass and seeing Beth, and Melinda, standing across the street talking.

The two of them were standing beside a mailbox. The window was very dusty but they were both standing so that I could see their profiles and I knew the moment my eyes focused on them who they were. Very slowly I lowered my arm back down to my side. Melinda was wearing her hair up on top of her head the way she had in the subway. She said something and Beth laughed. Then Beth said something, gesturing with her hands as she talked. A taxi stopped beside them in the street and a man got out and walked up onto the sidewalk. They moved over slightly so that Melinda was in front of the mailbox. Beth kept talking and laughed again.

Keeping my eyes on them, I reached down to unfasten the button in the center of the coat. I removed it, rested it over the back of the chair, then stopped a moment and reached out to try and rub away some of the dust on the window, but the dust was on the other side. I unfastened the pants and let them fall to the floor, stepped out of them, not taking my eyes away from the two girls; I picked up my own pants and pulled them on, put my feet into my shoes, then bent over and tied them.

I grabbed the summer suit and opened the door again and hurried down the stairs with it. The man who had measured me was standing at the bottom, smiling and holding his hands together in front of him. "Well now," he said as I reached him, "just how did it strike you on?" I handed him the suit, ran past him and out the front door. They were gone. I ran partway to the corner, then cut in between two cars, jumped past another, then stopped on the white line, waiting for one to pass the other way. A car honked, I ran the rest of the way across the street and between two cars and up onto the sidewalk beside the mailbox. I looked down one sidewalk, then the other. I stood on my tiptoes to look over people's heads but didn't see either of them. I turned around and looked the other way. A man carrying a brief-case walked by and jostled me. I looked across the street, up to the second floor of the clothing store. The small dusty window was there and another one beside it and another beside that. I lowered my eyes to the first floor. The man who had measured me was standing in the doorway, holding the summer suit over one of his arms, looking across the street at me.

I looked down at the cement of the sidewalk. It was exactly where I was standing that I had seen them. I glanced at the mailbox, then back down at the crack in the cement underneath my feet. I looked at it for quite a while; then I turned and started walking back toward the travel agency.

There was a note scotch-taped to the glass of the door when I got there and also a customer, who got there just as I did, went up and tried the door, yanking at it a few times after finding it locked. He turned and looked at me. "What kind of place is this," he said. "Can you tell me?"

I had been reaching out to remove the note from the door. I withdrew my hand.

"Can you?"

"What do you mean."

"I mean what is a travel agency doing on one of the busiest streets, the best locations, if you can't even count on them to be in here during the times they say." He turned toward the door again and indicated some small decal letters on the glass. "Nine until five-thirty."

I bent forward to look at the letters. "Oh yes."

"That's right," he said. "And what time is it now?" He pulled back his sleeve, looked at his watch and then held it out for me to see. "See that?"

"Oh yes."

He let the sleeve go back over the watch. "I'm disgusted," he said. "For the past three days I've come here at different times. Not once has there been anyone here. Is this your first time?"

"I've been here before."

"Take a clue." He reached out and put his hand on my arm. "Take a clue, son. Find another travel agency; this place is hopeless."

"I may do that."

He turned and walked on down the sidewalk. I waited till he was several stores away, then reached up and took down the note.

It was folded in half, written in pencil on an old memo pad, with Becker Travel printed across the top of it.

DEAR ROGER,
Missed you. Did you get the suit? There is a shoe store down two blocks and over one where I will be for a while.
LOVE,
BETH

There were two shoe stores near the travel agency. One had both men's shoes and women's shoes and the other one was a smaller one with just women's shoes. I started down the sidewalk, stuffing the note in my pocket as I walked.

When I got to the store I stepped just inside and stopped. A man came up toward me, glanced at my shoes, then at my face. "How do you do?"

"How do you do." I looked back into the store at customers sitting in chairs, salesmen sitting in front of them putting shoes on their feet. "I'm looking for a girl," I said.

Keeping his hands behind his back, the man turned and looked back into the store. "Young?"

"About my age."

"Attractive?"

"I think you could . . . yes."

"It doesn't appear that any of our customers fit that description at the moment."

"Thank you." I walked out of the store and started down the sidewalk again.

The other shoe store was around the corner. There was a table in the entranceway covered with shoes and a sign in them reading Spring Sale. I walked inside and saw Beth at the other end of the store.

She was standing in front of a low mirror and looking

down at her feet. On them were a pair of low-heeled orange shoes. I put my hands in my pockets and walked through the store toward her. A woman was a few yards apart from her, also looking down at the shoes. "I think they're right," the woman said, "do they feel right?"

Beth turned the other way, still looking down at the reflection of the shoes. "They seem to."

"They're really right," the woman said.

Beth stepped a few feet back from the mirror. "I wonder if I could see the darker ones again." She glanced over at the woman, then saw me. "Oh."

"I got the note."

Beth bent over and removed one of the shoes. "Did you get the suit?" She held out the shoe. "How do you like this."

I took it, looked at the top of it, then turned it over. "Good," I said. "I have something to ask you."

The saleslady was still standing there, looking back and forth between us.

"Could I see the darker ones again?"

"Of course." She turned and walked away.

"Really cheesey," Beth said. "Look here." She took the shoe back and ran her finger along the seam between the leather of the sole and the orange leather of the shoe. "Glue."

I looked down at it.

She pulled at it. "It's already starting to come apart a little."

"Don't get them."

The saleslady was over at the wall pulling down boxes. She came partway back with one of them in her hand. "Did you want to see the olive ones again?" she said. She opened the top of the box and showed them to Beth.

"I'll look at them."

"The girl who should be waiting on you just left this morning," the lady said. "No notice. Nothing. That's why things are so chaotic." She put the top back on the box, then turned around and went back to the shelves.

"I don't know how to put this," I said.

Beth bent over and put the orange shoe on again and set her foot back down on the rug. She looked at her feet in the mirror. "Oh guess who I bumped into today on the sidewalk," she said. She turned the other way.

"Who."

The lady was walking back with two boxes. "These are the ones you wanted," she said.

Beth sat down on a chair beside the mirror and reached down to remove her shoes. The lady got down on her knees beside the chair and removed a pair of dark orange shoes from one of the boxes.

"Who," I said.

"Do you remember the girl I told you about on the plane?"

"Which girl."

"You remember I told you about the trip from Chicago to Boston."

"Yes."

The lady had fitted one of the dark orange shoes on. "Is that too short?"

"Let's see; no."

She lifted the other one out of the tissue paper in the box. "Let's try this one."

"The plane trip from Chicago to Boston," I said.

"You remember how I told you how upset I was, crying and so forth; right after I'd called Aunt Nell from the terminal?"

"Yes?"

The lady had the other shoe on the other foot. "Stand up and try those now."

Beth got up from the chair. "These are softer than the others."

"They're a softer leather."

She took several steps past the mirror, then took several steps back. "Are they glued or stitched."

"Glued *and* stitched."

"Right after the call to Nell," I said. "Crying on the plane."

"Sit down again," the lady said, "and let me show you something."

Beth seated herself on the chair and the lady got on her knees.

"Anyway, the girl who was in the seat beside me, the one who kept talking to me and telling me to calm down, consoling me. Didn't I tell you about her?"

"You just mentioned her."

The lady had removed one of the shoes and was holding it up to Beth. "You see? Stitched *and* glued."

Beth took the shoe and looked at it.

"Anyway," I said.

"It does seem more durable than the last pair."

"Oh they'll endure." The lady took the shoe and set it in the tissue paper again. "Let's look at these olive ones."

"Anyway," Beth said, "I ran into her today on the sidewalk; about two blocks down from your office."

The lady had removed the top from the second box. "These aren't olive," she said. "They're avocado."

"What was her name," I said.

"May I see those?" Beth bent over to look at them.

The lady removed one from the box. "Claudia left unexpectedly this morning," she said, holding it up. "We're in complete confusion."

Beth looked at the shoe. "I sort of like it. Is it durable?"

"Oh yes." She bent down to Beth's foot.

"The girl's name," I said.

"I never even found it out. All I know about her is that she was in Chicago looking for a job and didn't find one."

The lady removed the other shoe from the box and began fitting it on Beth's foot.

"Then she was on her way here to see someone. Today when I saw her she was on her way to the train station."

"Where."

"She was going back home."

The lady moved back. "Stand up on those now."

Beth got up from the chair.

"Home where."

Beth walked over to the mirror and looked down at the shoes. "I don't know. Somewhere in the South. She had a heavy southern accent." She turned the other way.

"Which train station."

"I don't know." She stepped several feet back from the mirror. "You know I like these; do you like these?"

I looked down at the shoes.

"I mean they're unusual," she said, "but I like them. I'm just wondering if they're durable."

"I've got to go." I turned around and ran out of the shoe store, knocking against the table of shoes on sale outside the door, then turned and ran down the sidewalk till I saw a taxi. I jumped in front of it and waved both of my arms up and down till it had stopped. Then I ran around to the side and pulled open the door and got in. "The train station," I said.

"Which one," the driver said.

"The closest," I leaned forward on the seat, "and for God's sake hurry, sir."

In one intersection was an accident, two cars stuck against each other directly in the center of the intersection. "Wreck," the driver said as we stopped. He twisted his head back and looked out the rear window. "Too late to turn around." I looked back through the rear window, then out

the front again. The driver opened his door and stepped
down into the street. I got out too. There was some glass on
the street and several policemen. "These cops," the driver
said, "they don't know what they're doing."

"How far to the station."

He stood looking out over the top of the accident for a few
minutes, then gestured off at an angle. "Ten blocks, maybe."

"Too far to walk."

He climbed back into his seat. "You don't want to walk."

I got back into my seat.

Finally a tow truck came, attached its hook to the bumper
of one of the cars and dragged both of them over to the side
of the intersection, the metal of the cars screeching loudly
against the pavement. We started forward, crunched over
some of the broken glass in the intersection, then drove ten
more blocks to the station. The driver pulled up at the corner by the entrance; I handed him two dollar bills, and got
out.

There is a passageway that leads into the main part of the
station, which is a huge room made of stone with dusty windows high by the ceiling. An information booth is in the
center room. I hurried across the marble floor and to a man
sitting in the booth. Several others were also crowding up
toward him. One woman was holding a box of animal
crackers in her hand, crushing it slightly and pushing in
against another woman in front of her. "What track for
Pinedale," she said.

"One at a time please," the man said.

Another man came up behind me and pressed forward
toward the counter. "Excuse me," he said, "do you have a
lost and found?"

The man behind the counter pointed off toward the corner
of the room, then lowered his arm again.

"Pinedale."

"Is there a four o'clock train to New Haven?" a woman said, pressing in from the side.

The man's hand moved under the counter, then came up with a schedule. He opened it, picked up a pencil with the other hand to make a mark with, then handed the schedule to the woman who had asked.

"What about Pinedale."

"I've never heard of Pinedale."

"Excuse me," I said, "is there a train going to the South."

An old man pushed in from behind. "I think I'm at the wrong station," he said.

"What station do you want."

"I'm not sure."

"A train to the South."

A woman came up carrying a laundry bag cinched at the top with a rope. "Is this the information booth?"

"I'm sorry to be pushy," I said, squeezing up till I was right against the counter, "but there's someone I have to find leaving on a train for South Carolina. Is there such a train?"

"Yes," the man said.

He opened his mouth again, but before he could speak a loud voice came out of a loudspeaker somewhere way up high in the room. "The Dixie Limited now departing on track four," it said. "For New York, Philadelphia, Washington, Charleston and points south."

"Thank you." I pushed back through the others. On the opposite side of the room from the ticket windows were the openings leading out to the tracks. I looked at the nearest one and at the numbers over it, that read 15. I looked to the next one, which was 14, then began hurrying along toward the front of the station, reading the numbers till I saw track 4 ahead. I ran through an opening and out onto the concrete platform by the tracks. A train was standing there, steam hissing up from under the car nearest me. Just as I came out a porter stepped down out of the train and bent over to pick up a small footstool by the door. "No! Wait!" I ran up to the train, stepped on the stool as he began picking it up, then climbed up the stairs just as the train jerked forward. There was another jerk, then it began forward again. I pushed open the door of the car and went inside. Two men were sitting in chairs smoking cigarettes. Across from them a man was reading a newspaper. I walked past them and past a boy who was helping an old woman lift her bag up onto the rack overhead. The train was moving faster, past a baggagemaster outside who was pushing a large empty baggage cart. I walked along the aisle, looking back and forth at the people seated in their seats. When I got to the end of the car I stopped and turned around and looked back at the passengers' faces. Then I pushed open the door between the cars, walked through the small passageway to the next car. Inside, another man was reading a newspaper and across from him a girl was removing a cigarette from a cigarette case. I walked pass them and started along the aisle, looking back and forth at the people in their seats. Halfway through the car a conductor was taking tickets, punching them and inserting slips of paper at the top of the seats. I stepped aside so he could pass. "Where are you sitting," he said.

"I don't have a seat yet."

He took a ticket from a woman in the seat beside us and punched a hole in it. "Where are you going."

"I don't know yet."

He reached into his pocket for a slip of paper and put it in the top of the seat in front of the lady. "Find a seat," he said.

"I will." I started forward, then stopped at the front of the car to look back at the faces of the passengers. I turned around, pushed open a door and stepped out into the space between the cars. The train was still moving slowly, but there was a loud clattering sound till I pushed open the door leading into the next car and walked through it.

Melinda was sitting nearly at the other end of the car, facing the other way. My eyes went to her the moment I stepped into the car and even though I could only see the back of her head I knew it was her. I put my hand against the wall to steady myself. For a long time I looked down the length of the car at the back of her head, rocking back and forth slightly with the motion of the train. Finally I looked beside me and at a small water faucet built into the wall. Beside it, in another opening was a dispenser of paper cups. I removed a paper cup, then held it under the faucet till water filled the cup. I drank it, then threw the cup away and removed another. I filled the second cup and started slowly down the aisle with it. Before I got to the other end, the train began to move more and more slowly and then we came into another station. With a loud squeaking noise and steam rising up beside the windows the train came to a stop. Outside several people hurried along in the direction of the train's door. When I was a few seats behind Melinda I stepped into one of the seats across the aisle and sat down. A woman came in with a paper sack and walked past me, then a sailor came in, glanced at Melinda, but walked on and took a seat in the center of the car. Melinda sat with her head turned slightly toward the window, looking out at a rusted track running along beside a stone wall. After we had been sitting a few moments I got up and moved up to be in the seat behind her, but still on the other side of the aisle. She had on a blue skirt and a sweater with a copy of *Life* magazine resting in her lap. After I had been looking at her for a few moments she lifted up one of her hands and wiped the back of it across her eye. Then she returned it to the other one on top of the magazine.

I didn't try and get her attention until the train began to move again. Finally there was a slight jerk, we began moving forward, there was another jerk, we began moving faster and gradually the station and some people standing outside moved on past the window. Carrying the cup of water, I got up, stepped across the aisle and seated myself beside Melinda. She was looking out the window. When she felt someone was sitting beside her she reached for her skirt and pulled it closer to her leg but didn't turn her face from the window. I turned in the seat and held the cup in front of her but still she didn't look around. The end of the platform passed by outside the window. We passed an enbankment then some green trees. Melinda's head turned and she looked down at the pointed cup of water in front of her. For several moments she sat looking at it, at the ripples moving outward across the surface of the water from the train's motion. Finally her head turned and she saw me. The train picked up more speed. Underneath the car the wheels clattered more loudly across the track. "Oh," she said.

"Here." I raised the cup of water up toward her face.

She looked at it, then back at me, then took the cup. She lifted it up to her mouth to take a swallow. I could see she was starting to cry again.

"Do you have a handkerchief?"

"No."

Just then the door in front of the car opened and a man stepped through it carrying a large metal basket, filled with candy bars and cartons of soft drinks. He started up the aisle. I turned and looked into the basket as he passed. On the side was a small package of Kleenex. "I'll take these." I reached into the basket and removed them.

"Twenty-five."

I reached into my pocket for a quarter and handed it to him, then tore open the package, pulled out one of the tissues and gave it to Melinda.

"Thank you."

"You're welcome."

She dabbed it against her eyes.

"You're sitting here," I said. "You're actually sitting right here."

"Yes."

"And you know Beth."

She nodded. "We were on the same plane from Chicago. I was going to come and see you. Then I found out who she was and I knew I couldn't." She crumpled up the tissue.

"Beth said you helped her. She said if it hadn't been for you she couldn't have made the trip."

Melinda was looking in front of her seat. "Wastebasket?"

"I'll take it." I took the tissue from her and put it in my pocket. "You were in Chicago?"

"I was looking for a job there. I couldn't find one. I went to a nightclub in New York to get a job as a waitress. They didn't have the job anymore. They told me to go to this club in Chicago and I could have a job. I went there but the job was taken." She took another sip of the water.

"What about Sal."

She shook her head.

"I tried to look him up in the phone book. I even started to drive down there once to find you, but I knew I never would have."

She finished the water and rested her cup and her hands on the cover of the magazine. "He didn't have an advertising company," she said. "He just had a loft down by some warehouses where he lived. He was designing an advertisement for a camera. Then he was going to take it up to the camera company and see if they liked it. He'd been working on it for seven months. I went into his loft and saw what it was and then when he was going to the bathroom I went out and never saw him again."

The conductor came to stand by our seat. Across the aisle a woman opened her purse, reached into it and handed him her ticket. Melinda lifted up her magazine. Her ticket was resting underneath on her skirt. "You're going back home then," I said.

"Yes." She picked up the ticket.

"Do you know what you'll do there?"

"No," she said, looking up at the conductor. "I had some beaux there."

"Beaux?"

The conductor reached over my hand and took her ticket. He punched it.

"Just because you couldn't find a job? You're going back?"

"I wasn't cut out for a job. I thought I was but I wasn't."

The conductor handed back her ticket.

"You're giving up then."

She returned the ticket to her lap. "It was unrealistic to think of having a job and a career."

The conductor had wedged a slip of paper into the seat in front of us. "Your ticket?" he said.

I looked up at him. "I don't have one."

"How far are you going."

"I don't know."

He looked down at one of my shoes. "How far do you think you're going?"

"I don't know; what's the next station."

He rested his hand on the back of the seat. "Route One twenty-eight," he said.

"How much to there," I said, reaching into my pocket.

"Eighty-eight cents."

I removed a handful of change and counted out eighty-eight cents to hand to him. "If I go farther, I'll pay more." He looked at the money in his hand and counted. "Station by station," I said. He stuck a ticket in the back of the seat in front of me, dropped the change into his pocket and moved on to the next seat. I looked back at Melinda. Her face was turned away and she had started to cry again. "Melinda."

"Could I have another Kleenex?"

I tore another one out of the packet and handed it to her. "You can't give up," I said.

"It was unrealistic."

"Listen," I said, turning in the seat to face her, "get off with me at the next stop. Come back with me. I know a place where there's a job for you."

She shook her head.

"Yes, Melinda."

She wiped at her eyes and then dabbed the Kleenex at her nose. She handed it back. "It's all over; I'm going home."

"Give me your ticket. I'll take it to the office tomorrow and get you a refund."

She sniffed.

"We'll get off; we'll go back. You'll have a job by the end of the day, and if not, you can get on the train again tomorrow and go home. All right?"

She looked down at her magazine. "What about this," she said.

"What's that."

"This magazine," she said, "I bought it to read on the train."

"Don't think of a magazine." I stood up. "Is this yours?" I said, pointing at the suitcase in the rack overhead.

"Yes."

I stepped out into the aisle, reached up and hoisted down the suitcase. "Bring the magazine. We'll wait up in front."

She stood and moved out into the aisle, then walked along behind me, sniffing and touching the Kleenex to her eyes. We squeezed past the conductor, then came to the door. I pulled it open and held it while Melinda walked through, then followed her onto a small platform between the cars. The top part of one of the doors was open. We walked over to it and I set down the suitcase. "You can never give up, Melinda," I said over the noise.

"Kleenex."

I tore out another tissue and handed it to her.

"You can never give up." I reached up and rested my hand on her shoulder. Outside several houses flashed by. Some trees went by. Then the train began to slow.

There was a very small station house at the stop, which was just a three-sided shed with a bench in it, then a phone booth beside it. Several taxis were parked in a parking lot. A porter opened the door when we stopped and set a small stand down on the asphalt. I took Melinda's arm and helped her down. I followed her, carrying the suitcase, and we walked past the station and to the nearest taxi where a driver was sitting, reading a newspaper. I opened the back door and helped Melinda in, then set the suitcase on the floor. "I'll make a call and be right back," I said. The driver folded up his paper to put on the seat beside him. "I'll be right back," I said. "Okay?"

"Sure."

As I walked back to the phone booth I felt in my pocket for my change and brought out a dime. I stepped into the booth, dropped it into the phone and dialed the number of my apartment. The phone rang several times, then was an-

swered by Beth. "This is Roger," I said. "I got Melinda off
the train."

There was a silence.

"You know her," I said. "It's the girl you know, from the
plane."

"Her?" Beth said.

"The same girl," I said.

"Well what's she going to do."

There was a hissing noise from the other side of the booth,
then the booth vibrated slightly as the train started moving
again. It picked up more speed; as the booth began vibrating
more there was a small buzzing noise in the light over my
head.

"She's very upset," I said, "about not finding a job." The
end of the train passed by the phone booth and the buzzing
noise over my head stopped, even though the booth continued to vibrate. "I didn't talk to her much; I just wanted to
get her off the train." The phone booth stopped vibrating.
"We're coming back," I said. "I told her I'd help her get a
job."

"The shoe store," Beth said.

"What is it?"

"They want someone in the shoe store."

The taxi beside Melinda's pulled out of the parking lot and
down the street.

"Do this," I said. "Go back to the shoe store. Tell the lady
you spoke to a friend of yours who might be willing to take
the job. But make it sound like you're doing them a favor,
not like she needs the job. Make it sound like she'll come
over and she might take it if it looks good. Make sure no one
else takes it; all right?"

"I'll go over now."

"We'll be there in half an hour."

Melinda was sitting in the back seat looking down into her

lap. In the front the driver looked up as I approached and reached back to push the door open a little farther. "Where to," he said as I climbed in.

"There's a shoe store downtown," I said. "Take us over there and I'll tell you where to go."

He pulled the door closed, turned around and put the flag up on his meter.

"I shouldn't have gotten off the train," Melinda said.

The driver started up his motor, turned the steering wheel and started toward the exit of the parking lot.

"There's a shoe store where Beth bought some shoes," I said. "They need a person."

Melinda shook her head.

The driver turned out into the street.

I looked down at Melinda's hands in her lap, then reached over and took one of them. "You can do it, Melinda," I said quietly.

"I can't." She turned her face away and lifted the Kleenex up to her eyes again.

"You *can*, Melinda." I squeezed her hand, then glanced up to see the driver watching us in his rearview mirror. He looked quickly away, then turned a corner and pushed down on his accelerator.

Beth was standing in front of the shoe store in her new shoes when we drove up. The taxi stopped and the driver reached back to open the door. I paid him, then stepped out and lifted out Melinda's suitcase. Beth came over beside us. I reached in and took Melinda's hand and helped her out, then pushed the door of the taxi closed. The three of us walked up onto the sidewalk and I set down the suitcase. Melinda was looking at the shoe store. She shook her head. "I don't want to," she said.

"Did you speak to the woman," I said to Beth.

"I told her what you said."

"Good," I said, "give me this." I took the *Life* magazine away from Melinda.

"What about this," Melinda said. "What if I waited till to-morrow. After a night's sleep."

"There's another girl who came for the job who might be back later," Beth said. "That's what the woman said."

I lifted up the suitcase again and carried it across the side-walk. Then I walked back. "Do this," I said. "Go in, say you heard there was an opening. That's all. Let her do the rest of the talking." A woman stopped at the shoe table in front of the store and moved her hand around among some of the shoes there.

"Oh God," Melinda said.

"Go on." I took her elbow and moved her toward the door.

"Wait."

"Right now," I said. "Go in and do it." I pushed her.

She took several steps, but then stopped again. She turned around and looked at Beth.

"Go on," Beth said, "you can do it."

After waiting another moment she turned around and walked past the lady rummaging around through shoes on the table and in through the door.

Beth and I walked over to the other side of the sidewalk to stand beside the suitcase.

"Why do you think she's had so much trouble," Beth said.

"I don't know." I tipped the suitcase on its end. "Do you want to sit?"

"No."

"I'll sit." I seated myself on the end of the suitcase and looked down at the cover of the *Life* magazine. "Maybe it's the southern accent."

Beth bent sideways so she could look in through the glass of the shoe store. "She's talking to her."

I leaned forward and looked through the glass and over the shoes displayed in the front window. Melinda was at the far end of the store with the woman. The woman was speaking to her and gesturing. "I think she loses her confidence," I said. "When it comes right down to talking to someone I think she loses her confidence. Either she starts apologizing for herself or comes on too strong. I mean that's just a guess." There was a large glass window in the front of the shoe store, then a strip of marble running up from the sidewalk, then a large glass window in the front of the next store. The suitcase was resting just in front of the strip of marble between the two windows. I leaned back against it and looked down at Beth's shoes. "How do they fit," I said.

"They fit well," she said, "but I might dye them. I mean I like them, but avocado doesn't go with anything I have."

"Are they durable?"

She raised one of her feet up behind her and pulled the shoe off. She handed it to me. "You can't really get a durable woman's shoe," she said. "Nurses' shoes, of course. Those last forever."

I looked at the seam between the sole and the green top part. "Hastily made," I said.

"There's nothing you can do about it."

I handed it back. "Just walk carefully."

Beth worked the shoe back onto her foot, then glanced into the shoe store again. "She's coming out."

I got up off the suitcase and took a step in front of the window. Melinda was walking down the aisle in the center of the store, the woman still standing in the back. Melinda reached up to wipe one of her eyes with the back of her hand. "Oh no," I said.

The woman in front was still shuffling through the shoes on the table. Melinda walked quickly out the door and past her, keeping her head down and looking at the sidewalk. She walked toward us. Beth stepped forward and I stepped forward at the same time. Beth held out one of her arms; I held out one of mine. "Well?" I said.

Tears had begun to stream down Melinda's face. "I got the job," she said.

Beth put her arm around Melinda's shoulder. "You got it."

"I got the job." She reached up and tried to wipe at the tears. "I start tomorrow."

I picked up the suitcase in one hand and put my other arm around Melinda's shoulder. "You got the job."

Beth kept her arm around Melinda from one side and I kept mine around her from the other as we started walking in the direction of the apartment, Melinda crying most of the way.

When we got up the stairs of the apartment I went ahead to open the door. Melinda came in after me, then Beth. I set down the suitcase. "Do you want to wash up or anything?" Beth said. "This is the bathroom." She walked to the door of the bathroom and pushed it open.

"Thank you," Melinda said.

"You'll stay here with us," I said.

Melinda looked at me a moment longer, then at Beth. "The three of us?"

"I'd like you to," Beth said.

Melinda looked back at me.

"Please," I said.

"I could think about it," she said. After a moment she turned and walked into the bathroom, closing the door after her.

Beth went to the refrigerator and opened it. She looked

inside, then removed a dish of ice cream with a spoon in it. "She's nervous about staying," she said.

"I can see that."

She took a bite and walked over toward me.

"It's the sex," I said, glancing at the bathroom door. "She doesn't know how that would work out."

"How would it." Beth raised another spoonful of the white substance to her mouth.

"I don't know." I took the dish from her and the spoon, took a bite of ice cream and handed them back.

"Maybe you should go in the bedroom with her when she comes out," Beth said.

"What would you do."

"I'd find something."

Beth took another bite of ice cream. When she was through I took the cup and spoon from her, had a bite, then handed them back. Water was running in the bathroom.

"I could try," I said. "I mean as it is it's awkward."

Beth dipped the spoon into the ice cream another time. "I noticed that."

When Melinda came out she had washed her face. Beth had finished the ice cream and was walking back toward the kitchenette. She set the dish in the sink. Then she turned on the water and began washing the spoon. "Did you find the soap?" I said to Melinda.

"I did."

Beth continued to wash the spoon; first the front, then the back, then the front again.

"We had some ice cream," I said.

"Oh?"

"Yes."

Beth turned off the water. She picked up a dish towel and began drying the spoon.

"So," I said, "why don't we go into the bedroom." I gestured at the bedroom door.

Melinda looked at the door, then glanced at me, at Beth and back at the door. She walked over to it and through it. I walked in after her, then pushed it closed, not all the way so that the latch clicked but just so that it was ajar.

There was a single bed with a table beside it and a clock on it. Beside the clock were three hairpins.

I cleared my throat. "I don't know if there's anything to say," I said. "Do you . . . want to stay with us?"

Melinda was standing looking at the bedside table.

I walked past her and to the bed. I reached down and touched the bedspread. "Do you?"

"I don't know." She took two steps over toward the bed, then stopped. "I never thought of myself in that kind of a situation."

"I never did either."

In the other room there was the sound of Beth's footsteps crossing the room.

"Do you think Beth ever did?" Melinda said.

"I don't think so."

There was the sound of a squeaking spring in the next room as Beth sat down on the couch. A moment later there was the sound of a page being turned. "She must be reading your magazine," I said.

The only sound in the bedroom was the humming of the electric clock on the table.

"I mean if it doesn't work it doesn't work," Melinda said. "That's really all it comes down to, isn't it?"

"I think so."

She took another step toward me, then reached up behind her neck and pulled her sweater over her head. She set it on the end of the bed. I reached out and unbuttoned the top button of her blouse, then the next and the next. There was the sound of another page turning in the next room. Melinda unfastened her skirt, then stepped out of it and rested it on the end of the bed with her sweater. I took off her blouse.

"I mean it's absurd not to try things," she said.

"I think that's right." I pulled down the covers.

Melinda reached behind her to unfasten her bra, then removed it and set it on the bed. She stepped out of her underpants, then took off her shoes. She walked to the bed and got in, seating herself with her legs crossed and her hands resting in her lap.

I undressed quickly, leaving my clothes and shoes on the floor, and got into the bed. Beth got up and walked across the living room to the kitchenette. The water at the sink was turned on for a few moments, then turned off. Then the sound of her footsteps going back across to the couch and the sound of the spring squeaking and the sound of a page turning. I helped Melinda down onto her back and moved over on top of her.

6

THE TELEGRAM was there the next morning at nine, under the door of the travel agency. I unlocked the door and pushed it open. At first I didn't see the telegram but stepped on it instead, then bent over to pick it up. I pushed the door the rest of the way open and stuck the rubber doorstop underneath it, then walked across the room to the desk, opening the yellow envelope. I sat down and pulled out the sheet inside, glancing down to the bottom first to read the name of Paul Becker. I started in at the top.

DEAR ROGER   HAVE SUFFERED RELAPSE   ANOTHER MONTH BE-
FORE MY RETURN   BRITISH HEART SPECIALIST HERE SAVED
MY LIFE   HAVE TO DEVOTE FULL ATTENTION TO HEALTH FROM
NOW ON   TRAVEL SERVICE TOO MUCH TO HANDLE   HOPE YOU
WILL TAKE OVER   UPON RETURN WILL TRANSFER FULL OWN-
ERSHIP AND MANAGEMENT TO YOU   PLEASE WRITE TO PRINCE
EDWARD HOTEL, CEYLON   YOUR VERY GOOD AND GRATEFUL
FRIEND, PAUL BECKER

I read it twice, then set it down on the desk. I must have sat for about five minutes. Finally I opened the drawer to remove a sheet of stationery. I started to wind it into the typewriter, then stopped, wound it back out and set it on the blotter. I reached to the far side of the desk for a pen. There was an inkwell at the corner of the desk. I opened it, filled the pen, then closed it and pulled the chair up closer to the desk to write.

DEAR MR. BECKER,

It is of course a severe blow to me to hear of your misfortune. The telegram was here this morning upon my arrival and I am stunned by it. There seems little to say. I only hope the British heart specialist is as competent as you seem to feel he is. If there was anything I felt I could do in the matter, I certainly wouldn't hesitate. Please let me know if there is anything here, such as gardeners at your home or anything like that, that I can help out with.

As far as the travel agency is concerned I would prefer to wait till your return before taking over its ownership and management. If it's necessary for you to step down I will consider it an honor and privilege to carry on with the work you started. The only reason I feel unwilling at this time to say I will do so is that I hope that you will be able to resume, to some extent, your work here, upon your return. If not, I will carry on here to the best of my capabilities.

My best to your wife. My thoughts are with you.

ROGER

I read it over, then opened the drawer for an envelope and addressed it to Mr. Paul Becker at the Prince Edward Hotel. Then I stamped it and sealed it, carried it outdoors and down the sidewalk to the mailbox, then walked back.

When I stepped back in through the door I noticed a cigarette butt that had been ground out on the carpet. I picked it up and carried it to the ashtray. There was also a crumpled brochure on the floor. I picked it up and carried it to the wastebasket, which was overflowing, then carried the wastebasket into the back room.

It took three hours to clean the office completely, dust the desk and filing cabinet, wash the windows and arrange things neatly. No customers called or came in while I was doing it. The last thing I did was to open the desk drawer for

some scotch tape, carry it to the wall and tape the corners of
the Taj Mahal poster back against the wall again. Then I
put the tape back in the drawer and went down the sidewalk
to the coffee shop to have lunch.

It was while I was sitting on the stool, after I had ordered
a cheeseburger and a piece of pie, that the idea of the new
house came to me. I thought of it all during the meal. Af-
terward, I walked back to the office and to the phone book
which was in the desk drawer. I pulled it out and opened the
yellow pages to the real estate section. I looked through all
the different realtors, then called one and made an appointment.

The house we had the appointment to see was in Brook-
line and we got there just after five-thirty in the afternoon.
The realtor was already there. I drove the car in through
the opening of a low stone wall and across the gravel driveway. Mr. Hansen was standing beside his car. I parked behind him and got out, pulling the front seat forward so Beth
could climb out from the back. Mr. Hansen walked forward.
"How do you do," he said.

I closed the car door after Beth, then shook his hand. "I'm
Roger Hart," I said. "That's Melinda over there; and this is
Beth."

"My pleasure." He glanced at Melinda, on the other side
of the car, then at Beth, then put his hands in his pockets.
"Well then. Shall we go inside?" He started up the walk
ahead of us. "Mr. Hart, I believe I told you on the phone I'd
have to get right back."

"You did."

He removed the keys from his pocket as we approached
the front door. "Why don't I just go along in a minute and
let you close the place up."

"Fine."

He inserted the key in the lock of the door, turned it and pushed open the door, then stepped aside. "My partner's ill today," he said to Beth as she passed him.

"I'm sorry."

Melinda went in next, nodding at him as she passed him, then I went in. When I was inside he removed his key from the lock and came in and closed the door. "The house is in excellent shape," he said. "You can see that for yourself."

"It's huge," Melinda said.

Beth walked over to an arched entrance of a living room. "Do all the carpets come with it?" she said.

"All of them."

She stepped into the large living room, looking off across gold carpet.

Melinda walked to the foot of a large curving stairway. "Can I go up?"

"Your second floor is up there," the realtor said, "then go on up to the next story and there's another bedroom and bath." Her hand on the dark wooden railing, Melinda started up the carpeted stairs.

Mr. Hansen turned toward me. "What was the name of your travel agency?"

"Becker," I said, "but it's going to be changed to Hart."

He gestured for me to go ahead of him. "Let me show you the kitchen and maid's quarters." We started walking through the hallway and around past the base of the stairs.

I walked into a large kitchen. These are all new appliances," he said. "Built-in refrigerator, cupboards. Garbage disposal of course." He walked over to the oven and opened its door. "Self-cleaning oven of course."

I nodded.

He closed the oven door. "No bugs in this kitchen."

"No."

He walked to a door on the other side of the room and opened it. "Maid's quarters through here." I followed him in through the door and down a short hall. "Bathroom," he said, opening one door as we passed it. "Bedroom down here at the end." We walked into the maid's room at the end. He raised a blind up over the window. "Very nice view of the backyard out here."

"It is nice," I said, looking out. "I don't think we'll have a maid, but it's nice."

He closed the blind again. "It could be used as a child's room just as easily." He walked back through the door and started down the hall again. Then just as we approached the open door to the bathroom, he stopped and turned partially back. "I'm sorry," he said, looking down at the floor, "I didn't . . . which one of the two girls was your wife. I didn't . . ."

I looked back at him but didn't answer.

"The two girls," he said.

"Yes."

He gestured out toward the other part of the house. "The blonde and the brunette."

"The blonde is Beth. The brunette is Melinda."

"Yes," he said, "is one of them your wife?"

"No."

He continued looking down at the floor. "Well that's what . . . I didn't . . ." He cleared his throat. "I thought . . ."

"Is there a good furnace in the house?"

"Oh yes," he said, looking up, "nearly new. Less than two years old. Come this way." He led me back into the kitchen again and toward a door leading out to the driveway. There was another door just before that, which he opened. Stairs leading down into a basement. He reached onto the wall just beside the door and turned on a light.

"I don't want to keep you," I said.

"No," he said. "Here." He removed his wallet from his pocket, opened it and removed a card.

"Thank you."

"The office is about five blocks from here." He returned the wallet to his pocket. "I hope you'll stop by when you're through. I should be there in twenty minutes."

"Good."

I took a step down the stairs.

"I don't usually leave people in a house," he said. "I never would have done it if I hadn't thought from our conversation . . ."

"We'll see that it's locked up tight when we go."

He started toward the back door, then stopped again. "One last thing," he said, looking down at the doorknob on the back door. "Let's see. The three of you. The three of you are interested in buying a house together."

"Yes."

"Right." He turned around. "You'd all buy it and all move in, is that it?"

"We'd planned to."

He took a hold of the open door of the basement. "Yes," he said, "well tell me this; do you mind my asking?"

"Not at all."

"Tell me this," he said, "the blonde girl . . ."

"Beth."

". . . and the brunette . . ."

"Melinda."

"Yes," he said, "Beth and Melinda and you . . ."

"Roger."

He looked up to smile. "Yes," he said, "Roger. Are the three of you, are any of you related in any way?"

"No," I said, "we're just friends."

He looked down at the level of my belt and began nodding.

"Good," he said, "I hope you'll stop by." He held out his hand. "Take your time; look around all you want."

I shook his hand.

"It was my pleasure to meet you," he said, "all of you." He turned around and went out the back door.

I started down the steps to the basement.